ALL THIS

Stories

JON ANDERSON

ALL THIS

First Printing, 2026

Trade Paperback ISBN: 979-8-9936461-0-7
eBook ISBN: 979-8-9936461-1-4

If anyone asks you who wrote down this song
Tell 'em Jack-the-Rabbit
Done been here and gone

TABLE OF CONTENTS

ALL THIS

For the third day in a row, Dave and I have spent six hours bumping through sandy tracks. We are tired, sore, sweaty, and covered in dust.

At dusk, we pull into the village of Gourma, in Northern Mali, and go straight to Amadou's house. Like many of the other buildings in this sparse place, it's a small one-room mud building with a makeshift veranda. Amadou, one of our field agents, meets us dressed in a red sweat suit with a logo from Altoona High School in Pennsylvania. He is wearing worn flip-flops and, even though it is getting dark, sunglasses.

The one-room house is small and dominated by a recovered cable spool that serves as a table. In one corner is a bed—a rectangular wooden frame sitting on four large stones with only a straw mat and a sheet. Amadou sits on the bed while we take the only two chairs in the house. The chairs are metal frames with plastic weaving.

On the wall above the bed is a calendar from three years before—it shows goods from a hardware shop in a town nearly four hours away. Near the bed are a well-worn issue of *Jeune Afrique*, and a frayed and coverless copy of "*Ambiguous*

"

Adventure." In a corner, there is a small charcoal grill, two blackened and dented aluminum pots, a small metal teapot, two small glass tea cups, and several mismatched spoons and forks. There is no electricity for 180 miles. Water comes from a well 300 yards away. A roofless outhouse is 15 yards away.

As it gets dark, Amadou lights the kerosene storm lamp and places it on the table. We exchange news and talk about the project.

Finally, Dave says, "It must be very difficult to live here."

"Yes," Amadou says, sweeping his hand expansively around the room. "Not everyone has all this."

MARKERS

Here—small circular scar on forehead. 1960. Fell against a dresser. Stoneyhaven, NY.

Palm of left hand—a small semi-circular scar. 1964. Playing in a woodpile with best friend, threw a board away but it had a bent nail, punctured the hand. Seven stitches. It was the weekend. Doctor said, "I had to come in for this?" Stoneyhaven, NY.

Side of right big toe, small bump. 1965. Stepped on something while wading in the shallows. Still itches. Great South Bay near Old Inlet.

Right forearm, a small circular scar. 1974. Tried to grab a friend from behind not realizing he was smoking a cigar. Dakar, Senegal.

Both ankles and lower calves, small purple circular scars—3 on left, 4 on right. 1977. Tropical ulcers (also known as "jungle rot"). Later, a friend would ask if I had been shot with buckshot. When my father saw them, he said, "Don't let your mother see that." Okandja, Gabon.

Left eye, small wriggly line on the white of the eye. 1978. Remnants of a loa-loa worm. Libreville, Gabon.

Right pelvis, a 2-inch scar. 1985. Had to lay down the Yamaha 200 to avoid hitting a kid. Bamako, Mali.

Here—Upper right calf. 1987. Muffler burn from Yamaha 200. Bamako, Mali

Under-forearms, both arms. Faint scars. 1988. Hit a cow on the Yamaha 200 and skidded across the asphalt with arms out. Bamako, Mali.

Right cheek. Slight redness. 1995 to present. She touched me. Worcester, MA.

Dark spots. Notably on face and arms. Some look like scabs. Some look like small ancient maps of lost continents. Some look like they might hurt. They come but never go. Just accumulating. Like the rings of a tree—you could tell someone's age by counting them. 1996—present. Everywhere I've been.

Here—Three small scars on right knee. 2005. Arthroscopic surgery. Washington, DC.

Faint scar left side of nose. 2015. Skin cancer removal. Washington, DC.

Small scar middle of back. 2017. Skin cancer removal. Washington, DC.

Here—Left shoulder tattoo of Picasso's Don Quixote. 2017. Result of being knighted by the Republic of Mali. Washington, DC.

Right shoulder tattoo of a Malian *chiwara*. 2018. *Chiwaras* are a symbol of perseverance. Washington, DC.

Here—left chest, deep scar in the shape of a life. 2020. She died. Everywhere.

Left wrist, 2-inch scar. 2020. Suicide attempt #2. Washington, DC.

Left cheek, faint scar. 2021. Skin cancer removal. Washington, DC.

RUNNING ERRANDS
IN THE BUSH

Uneven plywood table. Sticky plastic tablecloth. Big bottles of *Meuse*. We get the cold ones. Since there is no electricity, this means bottles that have been put into a bucket of water. They are perhaps one degree cooler than the ones coming directly from the crate. But we try to believe it makes a difference. The storm lamp on the table seems to throw more shadows than light. For a while, there is no one else but me and Pete. Congolese music playing on the radio. The one-armed, blue-eyed bartender dozes. Our truck is parked in the darkness outside.

Julienne comes in and asks about her bra. Then she asks us to buy her a beer.

But from where the truck is parked, there is a sharp, bright, and loud scream. Followed by, "What the fuck? What the goddamn fuck? Whose fucking blood is this?"

Pete looks calmly at me. "It's alive," he says.

Pete and Bill and I have gone into town. Ninety minutes away on a laterite track through the forest. Through occasional villages selling palm wine and smoked bushmeat. And kids running out to try and sell wild fruit and bananas.

In town, we go to the post office—*poste restante*—to see if our concerned mothers have sent us aerograms. They have. Our fathers have not written. But then, we have not written to our fathers. Bill has a letter from his girlfriend.

We go to the small store. We buy lots of sardines, macaroni, and tomato paste. This is our fallback meal. We fall back frequently. We buy bread. We buy nails and cement for work. We fulfill orders from our local families and friends.

- Please buy vegetable oil. Two liters.
- Please buy salt. And condensed milk.
- Nescafé.
- Get batteries. A box of Ds and a box of Cs.
- Get me 3 liters of kerosene.
- Buy storm lamp wicks.
- Get shotgun shells.
  - Don't you need a permit?
  - No, go to David's. He's behind the Mayor's office.
- Please buy perfume.
  - What kind?
  - "Love Me"
- I need a bra, extra-large. I will pay you back.
- Please buy me a gift.
  - Ok, what kind of gift?
  - Something nice.
- Get me notebooks and pens for school.

– What's your average?

– C+

– Ok. If you promise to get Bs.

– It's okay, you don't have to buy me anything.

We do the errands as best we can. Then we go to the bar. We flirt hard with the barmaid. We drink. They have a kerosene fridge and the beer is mildly cold. The bar has a record player and has one English 45. It's called "Believe in the Pill" by a group called Birth Control. It's terrible but it reminds us of home. We drink. Bill has gotten a Dear John letter. He drinks faster and deeper than Pete and me. We tell him, "fuck her." We buy him beers.

It's dark when we leave. Immediately outside of town, it's profoundly dark. A very deep and haunting dark. Bill is almost passed out. We help him climb into the bed of the truck so he can sleep. I drive, Pete next to me. The narrow laterite road weaves through the darkness, the road almost a tunnel.

As we go around bends, we hear Bill sliding around in the bed of the truck, sometimes knocking into the side walls. Pete asks me to slow down. He says, "I hope the tail gate is up," and laughs. We don't check. The villages are dark. Maybe one lantern in a doorway. It is quiet and dark.

I come around a sharp curve. In the road is a civet. A big one. He turns his masked face and freezes. I brake too late and skid on the laterite. I hit him. I come to a stop maybe 10 yards down the road. Since the rear lights are not good enough to see well, I back up trying to avoid the civet. Finally I see him again in my headlights. He is snarling and shaking his head. Baring his teeth. Salvia flies from his muzzle.

His hindquarters have been crushed. But he tries to drag himself across the road to the forest. We get out and walk toward him. He increases this thrashing. And his screaming.

I say "shit" and walk back to the truck and get the tire iron from behind the driver's seat. I've never done anything like this. I walk up to the civet. I look at Pete. He says, "Yeah, back of the head." I try and make sure to do it with one blow. Strangely, I'm successful. The civet—maybe 20 pounds—is finally quiet and still. Our local families will appreciate the meat. I pick the animal up and throw it into the back of the truck.

Back in Obili, we go straight to the bar. Julienne comes in and asks about her bra. Tomorrow we say. Distribution of orders can wait till tomorrow. She asks us to buy her a beer.

After the second beer, we hear Bill's scream from the truck outside.

HICKMAN BRIDGE

The young, energetic ranger at the station looks at him and says, "Maybe try the Hickman Bridge trail." The ranger smiles, or maybe smirks. The ranger knows; he has seen hundreds of old, small, deluded hikers this season. This one can be no exception.

Hickman Bridge—moderate hike—480 ft. change in elevation, canyon views, natural bridge, ruins, and petroglyphs. Some slickrock. 2.3 miles round-trip. 3.5 hours.

The hiker refuses the easy trails; not ready to surrender, to compromise, to admit, to acquiesce; not ready to give up. Yet he is too old for the "difficult" trails. He doesn't want to get into difficulty. He is moderate, grayish, average, mediocre, middle-aged. Actually, to be honest, past middle-age. When he was younger, he was perhaps not so mediocre, but now… Perhaps he was as mediocre but had more energy to hide it.

He leaves early, before most of the experienced hikers, the younger folks, the families and the older couples, who are not new to this, or are new to this. He seems to believe that by leaving early, the hike may be shorter, or fewer people will see him out of breath and struggling, or being early implies being organized and alert.

It is a simple hike and yet he has lots of worries. He might get lost. He might twist an ankle. His right knee, the one on which he had surgery, which has provided him with a coveted wealth of excuses, will give out. He is too out of shape to complete the hike. There will be ledges on steep cliffs, or ladders, or crawl spaces, or scrambling that he can't manage. The trail will be poorly marked. He does not want to turn back and admit defeat.

He paces himself. He used to think that this was a special skill of his. Now he wonders. Pacing is just a way to measure out his small, failed life, like a coffee spoon. Why should a person who was never in danger of burnout ever pace themselves? A way of measuring out the life of a person who could swell a crowd or two, of no significance. An extra.

It is cool and the canyon walls are blocking out most of the early morning sun. He hikes a steep incline through dry, open, rocky terrain. At an immense, rust-red sandstone wall, he stops and stares. The vertical wall must be 100 meters high. A couple goes by. She says, "It kind of makes you feel small, doesn't it?" He thinks, "Small*er*, smaller. It makes me feel smaller. I am already small."

He admires the immense wall's focus. Doing one thing well. Its verticality. Its being there. It is a lesson in focus. It has not wavered, nor had second thoughts. It has not been overcome by distractions. It chastens him and makes him envious. How to compare a life of a million compromises, of "decisions and revisions which a minute will reverse," to something that never changes, never doubts, is always focused.

He is still staring when later, a man goes by. "Is it speaking to you?" the man asks. He thinks, "Yes, it is speaking to me. But very quietly." He scrambles up the talus slope to get to the base of the vertical cliff. He looks around to see if anyone is nearby. He leans closer and puts his ear to the red sandstone. He listens. If there is a voice or a heartbeat, it is too slow and deep for him to hear. But as he listens intently, he finally hears something. Heartbeat of rock. But it is just the echo of his own small and tired heart. He steps back in shock. For a second, he thought he saw his face in the rock. A wrinkled, pale face, fading to white.

He is in an arroyo and climbs a bit up on the ledge and then back into the stream bed. He hikes down the stream bed and ends up where he left to climb up the side of the arroyo. He has gone in a circle and has lost the trail. Luckily, another hiker comes by on his way out. He says to the hiker, "I think I just passed this place." The man says, "Well, you just follow the stream bed upstream, you will be okay. The natural bridge is not far, just remember to make a sharp left as you come out from under the bridge." As he turns away he thinks he hears the other man guffaw. "And I have seen the eternal Footman hold my coat, and snicker…" He turns around and retraces his steps and rights himself on the trail, thankful for the chance passerby.

Just before the bridge, he encounters a young woman hiker who is tall and without a pack. He says hello but she passes without a word or a glance, proving his invisibility and insignificance. She is concentrated on other things. But he is surprised that she has no pack or water with her.

Finally, he arrives at the bridge, a large sandstone span carved out by a small, now dry, stream. Underneath the bridge, he sits and eats a peach. His rolled trousers have filled with dirt. The bridge seems not to know, and not to care, that he is there. He feels his life dissipate before him like sand running through his fingers, like a wave on the beach. His thoughts are just meaningless additions to the rubbish heap of small thoughts that make up his life. He struggles up and starts on the return trail.

It has gotten hot. At a fork in the trail that leads to a longer, more ambitious hike, he sees the woman hiker again and this time she is with a man with a pack. They seem to argue and she hikes off quickly in front of her partner.

On the way back, as he tires, his mind shrinks. He knows it happens but can't do anything about it. He becomes a zombie. He becomes less aware, his vision shortens to those steps in front of him. The horizon shrinks and he hears only his tinnitus.

Rounding a bend in the trail, he comes on a large boulder. The dark patina of the boulder is covered with scores of petroglyphs, hanging there like stars in the night sky. How did he miss this on the way in? The petroglyphs are like constellations floating in the sky. All the images seem discrete, as if there is no general theme, as if there were 100 different artists, each with their own vision. Some images appear to be rock sheep, some aligned in small flocks perhaps. There are newer ones with men on horseback. There are many handprints. There are strings of dots and broad-shouldered figures and long and twisting ladders like strands of DNA. I am here. I exist. Remember me. There are even newer ones: "Gonzalez 1954." Some pockmarks from bullets—bubbaglyphs. I am here. I have made a mark.

Three days ago, he heard a guide say that a visitor's guess about the meaning of petroglyphs was as good as anyone's. The images lift and drop a question on his plate. As good as anyone's. As good as the clerk at McDonald's. As good as the receptionist at Rodeway. As good as his own guesses. He thinks, "we are not drowning in our ignorance, we are bragging about it." Next to the petroglyphs is a small area of ruins, a partial stone wall built into a crevasse in the sandstone cliffs. A pile of washed-up and bleached bones on the shore of some tepid sea, where mermaids once sang.

He plods endlessly along the return trail. Finally, he sees the endpoint, the dark expanse of the parking lot. It has filled up since he left. He hears the voices of kids and families, guides and their groups, the familiar asphalt and noise. And, suddenly, he finds it hard to breathe.

THE GREEN SHOES

After washing and dressing in her best Sunday clothes, she sat on the bed and pulled the trunk closer. She unlocked it and pulled out a bundle. She unwrapped the bundle and, as every Sunday, her green shoes lay in their entire splendor.

The color of the shoes! No other shoes have this beautiful green. Like the fresh grass, the new grass at the end of the long dry season that the first rains give birth to out of the brown dust. That green that lifts your heart and gives you a smile—the shoes had magically captured that green. No other shoes in the world had quite this shade of green.

And the heels were so cleverly done. Not the heels on the young girls who stand on Mandela Avenue in the evening. No, not heels like that. But not heels like a wash lady, either. Heels that subtly underlined her attractiveness and her class, which demanded attention but not too much attention.

The straps were also not too thin and not too wide. Just right to show ladylikeness. And they had a nice gold buckle on the side.

She put the shoes on her wide brown feet. Sitting on the bed, she looked down at them. The green shoes fit perfectly.

Maybe her feet were a bit broad and bulged out a little, but the shoes fit perfectly anyway.

She was ready.

She opened her door and took off the shoes, closing the door behind her. She carried the shoes in her right hand and felt the warm, smooth earth on the soles of her feet as she walked to church.

She always got to church a bit early so she could put her shoes near the door. Everyone who came after her would see her green shoes near the door. They would wonder at how beautiful the shoes were and the special person who wore them!

At the end of the service, she stayed a bit longer and said an extra prayer. She asked God for forgiveness for spending most of the service praying that no one would steal her shoes. She knew they were hard to resist. And staying a bit longer gave the people who left before her time to pick up their brown and worn shoes and admire her green ones. She knew that God understood beauty and would forgive her.

Walking home, she switched the shoes to her left hand so Amadou, the shopkeeper, would be sure to see them. As she walked by, she sensed him looking at her. She kept her back straight and her head facing forward. But—maybe out of the corner of her eye—she saw him smile and maybe shake his head a little. She would not acknowledge him looking; she was too classy for that. She strode purposely home, the shoes dangling attractively from her hand. Maybe one day, Amadou would mention the shoes and then they would start a conversation.

When she got home, she sat on her bed and pulled her trunk closer. She put the green shoes on just to see her feet in them before putting them away. Then she took them off again, wrapped them in the cloth, and put them back in her trunk and locked it.

WOMAN ON THE SUBWAY
AT NIGHT

As always, I board at McPherson. But tonight it is much later than most nights. Around 9:30.

I sit on an inner-facing bench toward the end of the car, my pack between my legs. I exhale. The car only has a few passengers. Caddy-corner from me, at the very end of the car, behind a partial glass partition, sits a woman. She has long black hair and a pale complexion. She sits erect. She has large eyes. She is wearing a gray parka. Her thin and bare legs are crossed. Other than the parka, I can't see what she is wearing. Her legs are very long. She has on short boots with thick heels and three buckles on the side. She is drawing in a sketchbook. Every few moments, she glances at the partition and then back to her drawing. I watch her. Sometimes I think she notices and sometimes I think she is looking past me.

We ride like this for 27 minutes.

The conductor announces that we are arriving in Dunn Loring. The woman rips a page from her sketchbook and dumps the book in her bag. She takes the paper and folds it in half, then in half again, then in half again and then in half again. As we pull into the station, she stands and shoulders her bag. As the doors open, she walks toward the door. She stops in front of me. I look up. I'm surprised by how tall she is. She looks at me and smiles a little. She hands me the folded page and walks out through the open doors onto the platform. I hear the doors close behind her.

Slowly, I unfold the paper. On it is scrawled "Alice 703 928 9900 leave a message."

I fold the paper and put it in my pocket.

The conductor announces that we are arriving in Dunn Loring. The girl rips a page from her sketchbook and dumps the book in her bag. She takes the paper and folds it in half, then in half again, then in half again, and then in half again. As we pull into the station, she stands and shoulders her bag. As the doors open, she walks toward the door. She stops in front of me. I look up. I'm surprised by how tall she is. She looks at me and smiles a little. She hands me the folded page and walks out through the open doors onto the platform. I hear the doors close behind her.

Slowly, I unfold the paper. On it is written, in a very precise hand: "You seem interested and interesting. Bailey's Pub. Friday Night 9:30. In the back."

I fold the paper and put it in my pocket.

The conductor announces that we are arriving in Dunn Loring. The woman rips a page from her sketchbook and dumps the book in her bag. She takes the paper and folds it in half, then in half again, then in half again, and then in half again. As we pull into the station, she stands and shoulders her bag. As the doors open, she walks toward the door. She stops in front of me. I look up. I'm surprised by how tall she is. She looks at me and smiles a little. She hands me the folded page and walks out through the open doors onto the platform. I hear the doors close behind her.

Slowly, I unfold the paper. I turn it over. I bring it closer to examine it. It is blank.

I fold the paper and put it in my pocket.

The conductor announces that we are arriving in Dunn Loring. The woman rips a page from her sketchbook and dumps the book in her bag. She takes the paper and folds it in half, then in half again, then in half again, and then in half again. As we pull into the station, she stands and shoulders her bag. As the doors open, she walks toward the door. She stops in front of me. I look up. I'm surprised by how tall she is. She looks at me and smiles a little. She hands me the folded page and walks out through the open doors onto the platform. I hear the doors close behind her.

Slowly, I unfold the paper. It is a portrait of me, done in great detail. The same tie and jacket. The close-cropped beard. The short hair. In the portrait, my eyes and mouth are sewn shut.

I fold the paper and put it in my pocket.

The conductor announces that we are arriving in Dunn Loring. The woman rips a page from her sketchbook and dumps the book in her bag. She takes the paper and folds it in half, then in half again, then in half again, and then in half again. As we pull into the station, she stands and shoulders her bag. As the doors open, she walks toward the door. She stops in front of me. I look up. I'm surprised by how tall she is. She looks at me and smiles a little. She hands me the folded page and walks out through the open doors onto the platform. I hear the doors close behind me.

Slowly, I unfold the paper. On it is scrawled in large block letters: "Fuck you. Just *fuck* you."

I fold the paper and put it in my pocket.

The conductor announces that we are arriving in Dunn Loring. The woman rips a page from her sketchbook and dumps the book in her bag. She takes the paper and folds it in half, then in half again, then in half again, and then in half again. As we pull into the station, she stands and shoulders her bag. As the doors open, she walks toward the door. She stops in front of me. I look up. I'm surprised by how tall she is. She looks at me and smiles a little. She hands me the folded page and walks out through the open doors onto the platform. I hear the doors close behind her.

Slowly, I unfold the paper. On it is a very realistic drawing of a nude woman, facing forward. Her legs are shackled. Her hands are behind her back. Her head is covered in a hood.

I fold the paper and put it in my pocket.

The conductor announces that we are arriving in Dunn Loring. The woman perks up, but this is not her stop. She is going to the end of the line like me. She catches me looking at her. She smiles. She pulls her coat where it has overlapped with the seat next to her. She looks at me. While I am watching, she looks at the empty seat next to her and back at me. I get up and go over and sit next to her. As I get there, she closes her book before I can see what she has been drawing.

"Hello," she says.

"Hi," I say.

"You look tired."

"A bit," I say.

She says, "I can fix that."

The conductor announces that we are arriving in Dunn Loring. The woman perks up, but this is not her stop. She is going to the end of the line like me. She catches me looking at her. She smiles. She pulls her coat where it has overlapped with the seat next to her. She looks at me. While I am watching, she looks at the empty seat next to her and back at me. I get up and go over and sit next to her.

In the book is a very basic drawing of a large pink heart. I look at her closely. Her clear skin. Her large eyes. I suddenly realize that she is perhaps 12. As I rush to get up to leave, she says "No. Wait. Stay."

The conductor announces that we are arriving in Dunn Loring. The woman perks up, but this is not her stop. She is going to the end of the line like me. She catches me looking at her. She smiles. She pulls her coat where it has overlapped with the seat next to her. She looks at me. While I am watching, she looks at the empty seat next to her and back at me. I get up and go over and sit next to her. As I get there, she closes her book before I can see what she has been drawing.

"Hey," she says. "I thought you'd never come over."

"How long have you noticed?"

"Since you got on," she says.

She puts her hand on my knee.

"I can't wait," she says and closes her eyes.

The conductor announces that we are arriving in Dunn Loring. The woman perks up, but this is not her stop. She is going to the end of the line like me. She catches me looking at her. She smiles. She pulls her coat where it has overlapped with the seat next to her. She looks at me. While I am watching, she looks at the empty seat next to her and back at me. I get up and go over and sit next to her.

Loudly, she says, "What the fuck are you doing?"

She gets up quickly, pushes past me, and walks to the other end of the car and stands near the doors.

The conductor announces that we are arriving in Dunn Loring. The woman perks up, but this is not her stop. She is going to the end of the line like me. As we approach Vienna, I get up and take a hesitant step toward her.

As the train stops, I say, "Can I see?" My question happens at the same time as the conductor makes an announcement about this being the end of the line and to make sure you take all your personal items. The woman has not heard me. She closes her book, gathers her bag, and walks past me through the subway doors. I follow. I see her ahead of me walking toward the escalator. On the escalator, I am seven steps behind her. We go through the turnstiles at the same time; she is three down from me. We walk out into the open area. Without hesitation, she turns to exit on the south side. I stand in no man's land for a second. I turn and like a thousand times before, I go out the north side.

RESPECT

At the ceremony, I sit next to an old man in the front row. We do not have a common language, so we sit silently in the hot sun on the low chairs and pretend to listen to the speeches. He wore an old, faded *boubou* which had been carefully repaired and was freshly washed.

Periodically, a platter of grilled lamb would be passed down our row. The meat was delicious, especially when dipped in the salt mixture at the edge of the platter. Food at these types of ceremonies tended to go very fast. I got the impression sometimes that people only ate at ceremonies, by the ravenous way food was consumed.

I began to notice that the old man would never take any meat and always passed the platter directly on to me. For some reason this began to annoy me. As a young outsider, I did not want preferential treatment, especially, from older people who should be held in respect.

When the platter got to me for the fourth time, I held it back out to the old man. He shook his head and held out his hand in a gentle "no" gesture.

This then happened several times.

Finally, I had had enough. I held the platter back out to him. I was not to be deterred. I would not move it until he took a piece. He shook his head. I insisted. He held out his hand. I persisted.

Finally, he looked me in the eyes and slowly smiled.

He only had two teeth.

ALMOST PERFECT

As soon as Frank awoke and went downstairs, he saw a young, grubby kid at the door. In Bamako, kids replaced telephones—they seemed to be the most frequent means of communication. Kids were sent everywhere with all sorts of messages for all sorts of people—the poor man's cell phone.

In broken English and Bambara, the kid said that Penda was at the clinic. Frank gave the kid a quarter. He was fairly sure the kid was saying that Penda was at the clinic—he was never sure he understood Bambara correctly. Penda, a strong, healthy woman, was having her first child.

Frank drove to the maternity on his way to work. He wanted to be as useful as possible. Frank did this partly because the father of Penda's baby was not around, not providing support, obvious by his absence. So instead, Frank, her brother-in-law from worlds away, tried to pay the bills, the prescriptions, to be there in the room. He knew it was not the same—that there were limits to the type of help he could provide and to his knowledge of the cultural context of love.

The worn-out clinic had no electricity, no medicines, no materials, just three metal beds. The bottom halves of the cement walls desperately needed a cleaning and a paint job—the hands of thousands of people had been rubbed against it. The midwives were attentive and well-intentioned. Penda's pregnancy had already been long and hard—with several trips to the doctor. He was not sure the doctors she consulted knew what they were doing.

Frank felt a general resentment against the father, the clinic, the system that allowed these situations to develop and forced him into positions where he was unsure, impotent. He became angry and started to close off.

Penda was in full labor. She was sweating and breathing hard, but she smiled briefly before returning to her pain and exhaustion. He had to return to work, promising to be back as soon as he could.

The meetings went longer than he expected. It was several hours before he could return.

Anya, Penda's mother, was sitting on the veranda of the maternity, holding the baby. They shared only a few words in common, although they often spent hours together. Anya was the center of the family, holding together a loose coalition of her children and their children. She was the center of all major family events.

He could hear Penda crying inside. He heard the soothing mutterings of the midwives.

Anya looked up with sad and anxious eyes. Tenderly, she held out the baby.

"*A sara*," she said.

He didn't understand. He couldn't understand. The earth slowed, the universe stopped expanding, and his skin cooled.

He carefully took the quiet, peaceful baby girl. She had a full head of lush black curls. Her skin was smooth and brown as a shea nut. Her fingers and toes were perfectly formed. Her arms and legs were as plump as ripe mangoes. She was a big baby. Her eyes were closed.

She was beautiful, almost perfect.

POLICE REPORT

1. Heading

- **Police Department Name:** East Rock Precinct
- **Report Title:** Kidnapping, and Ransom attempt
- **Report Number / Case ID:** Pending
- **Date and Time of Report Filing:** October 14, 1984
- **Officer Name and Badge Number:** John Franz; 38392

2. Incident Details

- **Date and Time of Incident:** October 13, 1984
- **Location of Incident:** around 9783 Sider Drive, Newport
- **Type of Incident:** bboy, 10, abducted on his way home, from school.

3. Involved Parties

- **Victim(s):**
  - Full Name: Stevie James
  - Age: 10
  - Contact Information: Mother – Elizabeth James
  - Address (optional): 9323 Sider Dr.
- **Suspect(s):**
  - Full Name (if known): None
  - Description (height, build, clothing, identifiable marks): None
  - Last known location: None
- **Witness(es):**
  - Name and contact info: None
  - Brief statement (if applicable): None

4. Narrative / Description of Events

- Chronological account of what happened
- Actions taken by involved individuals: Mother searched street. Officer did also.
- What the reporting officer observed upon arrival: Went to home. Mother distraught. Crying. Waited for son who never arrived. Called school, and got confirmation, that bboy bboarded bbus.
- Evidence found or collected (e.g., photos, video, items): Ransom note, bbelow.

5. Officer Actions

- Response time: Arrived on the scene after Mother's 911 call at 3:35.
- Interviews conducted: Talked with Mother
- Evidence gathered: Collected a ransom note, from the parents. A scan, is attached bbelow.
- Statements recorded: Got statement, from Mother
- Arrests made (if any): No arrests at this point.
- Report of use of force (if applicable): BBoy was apparently taken by force, on the way home, from school.

6. Attachments / Evidence

- Photos: N/A
- Witness statements: Interviewed Mother.
- Diagrams or sketches (e.g., crime scene or traffic layout). N/A
- Video footage references: N/A
- Reports from other responding units: N/A

7. Conclusion / Disposition

- Summary of findings
- Next steps or recommendations (e.g., further investigation, case closed, follow-up): Asking for motive.
- Charges filed (if any): None

8. Officer Signature

- Officer's Printed Name and Signature /s/ John Franz
- Date: October 14, 1984
- Supervisor Review/Signature (if required): N/A

Attachment: Ransom note

Scan of the typed ransom note is below:

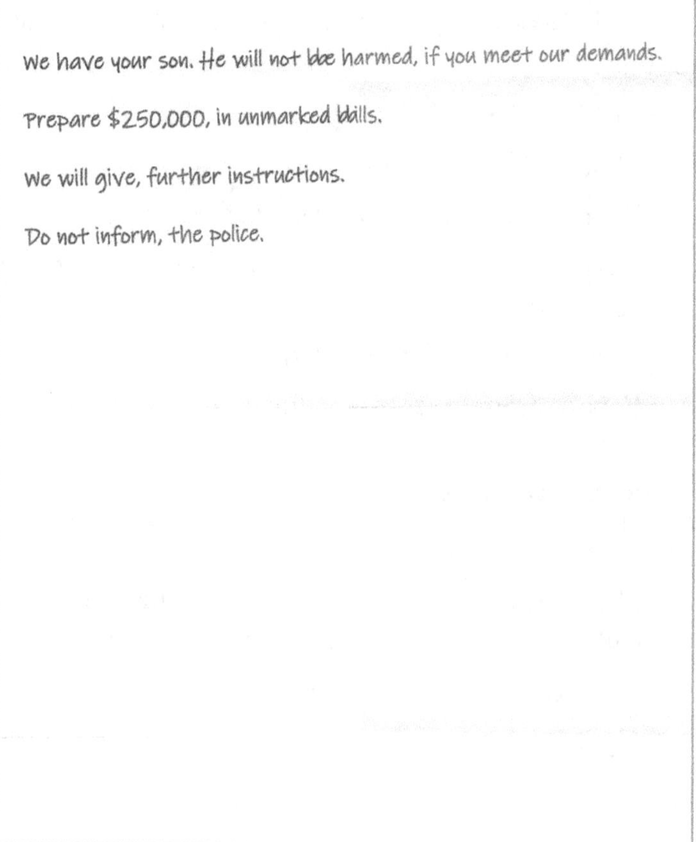

PRAYERS

My front door is open. I enter. There is no one on the first floor. On the dining room table are someone's hair, someone's bra, and someone's jeans.

I go upstairs. There is someone in the bathroom. They are standing on their right leg, with the other leg hitched up and are washing their left foot in the sink. Ablution.

I go back downstairs and settle on the couch.

The person comes downstairs and wraps themselves in a large thin cloth. They cover their head. In the living room, on the rug, the person begins to pray. Standing, bending over, kneeling, forehead to carpet.

Toward the end of the prayers, the person remains seated on the rug and mouths prayers, counting with her fingers.

I watch intently. As she silently prays, she turns and looks at me. As we stare at each other, the person slowly crosses her eyes.

CLOSE CALLS

Your friend's mom picked you up from basketball practice
And on the way home, the car swerved and
Ended up facing the wrong way on the median

You were a favorite of the older camp counselor
On a hiking trip, you were alone with him
He stood very close to you and wiped your forehead

The girl, third desk in the first row,
She was, in fact, interested in you
But you never said anything

On a dark day, you took the revolver
Out on to the marshes, walking for hours
But a bolt of lightning scared you home

As a toddler, you fell into the pool
Suddenly, Someone-Like-God yanked you out with one hand
"Look what I found," said Someone-Like-God

Your CV was not that good
There were better
But the evaluator thought somehow you were a "better fit"

Your life has been a series of close calls and near misses
Most of which you are not even aware of
The huge majority you are not even aware of

Some people never saw this poem
Some people stopped reading halfway through to attend to
an emergency
Hopefully it went okay

But you
Here you are
In spite of all the near misses and close calls
Here you are
Right here and right now

Congratulations

NAFISSA

The curtain that covers the doorway was intended to keep the sharp blades of heat from the room. We push it aside and it slumps closed behind us. We let our eyes adjust to the darkness. The small room has no windows. It is the only room in the house.

There is a woman sitting on a mat on the dirt floor. She is holding a child. In one corner of the room, on the floor, lay several pots and cooking utensils. In another corner is a worn-out trunk. The woman indicates two low stools for us to sit on. There is little else on the dirt floor or adobe walls, nor is there room for much else.

The little girl the woman is holding seems to be about 4 or 5, but it is hard to tell. Her hair is beautifully braided, each braid ending with a colorful plastic barrette. The child cannot speak. Her hands are curled and stiff, her fingers strangely bent. Her arms and legs are thin. She drinks from a cup held by the woman who, from time to time, gently wipes the drool from the child's mouth. The child has an enormous toothy smile and beautiful eyes. Her name is Nafissa.

She stares at us. She makes a random gesture. The woman says she wants to touch me. I hold out my hand and we touch. Her grin becomes wider. She is perhaps fascinated by my whiteness.

My wife, who knows the woman's family, asks where the father is. He has gone to Mopti. He left when it was clear that Nafissa had problems. The woman does not speak ill of him. There are no other relatives in a position to help. Some neighbors provide food. The doctors at the hospital claim it is a tumor and there is nothing they can do. Over the past 10 months it has gotten progressively worse. The woman does not complain. The woman does not seem unhappy. It's God's will, she says.

We tell the girl how beautiful she is. I tell her I will marry her when she is older.

We talk about acquaintances. About events. About relatives.

As we stand to leave, Nafissa squirms and looks at us with her huge eyes. I ask why she has become so animated.

"She wants to go with you," the woman says.

I take a long look at her and touch her cheek. "Next time," I say. "Next time."

We exit the hut. It's like walking into a fire—burning hot and bright. Our eyes try to readjust. The world shimmers in the heat.

THEY THINK

He learned a lot from Mali and his Malian friends. Not as much as he should have—he was stubborn and hard-headed. But Mali found cracks in the thick hide and once-shiny armor.

Some people think he has gone native.

But he realized he was not learning how to be a Malian. He was learning how to be a person. He learned the greetings and the constant handshakes, and he enjoyed it. The differences between copying and understanding, mimicry and knowledge. Everyone has their own rituals.

Some people think he has gone native.

But is not greeting people and shaking hands a social thing to do? A good thing to do? He learned that first you should always greet everybody. He learned that anyone could be your cousin, and directors were cousins of drivers, and the president could be teased by a doorman. And you, you could be told an uncomfortable truth by a cook and you could not get mad.

Some people think he has gone native.

He learned small lessons in dusty villages from people who had never gone to school, and with whom he didn't share a spoken language. He learned that there are other languages. He learned that the barefoot man in clean but worn clothes, with a fast and toothless smile, is the descendant of kings. In these slow, hot moments, he felt more real than before a thousand choices at the supermarket.

He learned that the "truth" may not be out there waiting for discovery and "uncovery" by clever people working alone. He learned that the truth might need to be constructed through dialogue, through conversations among large groups of different people, and it needed to be constructed and reconstructed every day. A good place to do this is under a big tree.

Some people think he has gone native.

He learned a level of stoicism and grace under difficulties. We are not our difficulties. We are how we deal with our difficulties. He wished he had learned this lesson better. Some people called it fatalism. But Malian mothers cry like other mothers.

Some people think he has gone native.

He learned that power is not binary with winners and losers, and the game of rock, paper, and scissors is more reflective of the world than a coin toss. He learned that honor is important and humiliation a terrible thing. He learned to always strive for respect, equity, and a just set of rules. A fight that's not fair is not a fight, and an unfair fight is not worth fighting, much less winning. He learned that small gestures count and the most generous people you will ever encounter are the ones who have much less than you. He learned he was an egotist, and a narrow-minded one at that. But he shook the fingerless hands of lepers and sat and joked with them. They drank tea. They laughed.

Some people think he has gone native.

He worked with Malian women whose interior courage extends beyond any horizon you will ever see. They have straight and strong backs, and big and inclusive hearts. They live in small villages, in small houses on dusty roads. They have babies and bury many of them in the sandy soils of the bush.

He learned, at least they tried to teach him, about tolerance, about not assuming you know another person's troubles.

He needed these lessons because the place he came from had not taught them so well. Sometimes they were not even in the lesson plan.

He was not a very good student. He wanted to do better.

But still, some people think he has gone native.

DUCKS AND BREAD

The smell of bread…

My mom was already sick but no one knew it but her. My daughter was three or four. They were not together very much. We lived in Africa and she lived in Stoneyhaven. On our visits, my Mom would take my daughter down to the old boat landing. There are old working boats there. Clam boats. Small fishing boats. Sail boats tied to faded wooden docks that creak and sway.

The boat yard was mostly empty but on some docks there were crabbers. Either older drunks or young kids. Rarely women. Rarely a healthy adult.

In the tall phragmites there is a dirt loop path. They walk along it together holding hands. My mom says that she needs the exercise. As if a five minute walk could hold off what was eating her. They have a bag of stale bread. At one end of the loop the phragmites open on to the water. Ducks live here. Mainly Muscovy and Mallard. Some as big as my daughter it seems.

They know my mom. They know why she is here. They do not know my daughter as well. They run up, squawking, pecking, lurching for the bread. My mom shoos them away from my daughter as she hides behind my mom's legs holding her pants.

A year later, my mom was dead.

Thirty years later, my daughter and I are driving to see my Dad. I ask her what she remembers about my Mom. "The smell of bread," she says. Later "and the ducks…"

THE PURPOSE OF TREES

We sit on woven reed mats on the ground under the shade of a neem tree. Since it must be 100 degrees and clouds have fled the pale, shimmering sky, we are thankful for the shade. With me is Cissé, a government-trained forester who speaks French, a traditional healer, and his apprentice. The healer is a Diakité and his apprentice a Coulibaly. Neither of them speaks French.

To begin, Diakité appreciates my somewhat scraggly beard. In return, I congratulate him on his even more scraggly beard—a few white hairs on the tip of his chin—of which he seems inordinately proud. His boubou is pale blue, clean, and a bit frayed. He has a small cap on. His bare feet are calloused and cracked. Coulibaly is slightly younger. He wears sunglasses with the sticker still attached to one of the lenses. He also has a thin, spare white beard. Cisse is much younger, has no beard, and has on green fatigues.

A teen makes tea on the porch, and every 20 minutes or so, he comes with two small glasses on a dented aluminum tray. He pours the tea from a small metal teapot in front of us. Since we must share the glasses, we insist the healers drink first. The glasses are quickly emptied and put back on the tray to be refilled for us. There are three sessions like this; each session the tea gets sweeter and, thankfully, weaker. Diakité is one of the tea drinkers who shows satisfaction through loud sips.

Cissé and I have organized an inventory of all the known different tree species from the Soussan National Forest. There are 63, give or take a couple. The inventory was mostly done by forestry students. Sixty-three is a good number and compares favorably to species richness in forests in the US. We have with us a plant press with specimens and also three books with either drawings or pictures of parts of different local trees. We hope to see if our conception of "species" corresponds with the local conception, and also to find out which trees have uses and what the uses are. Since much of traditional medicine is plant-based and healers spend significant time in the wild to collect material, it makes sense to work with well-known traditional healers.

We go one-by-one through our list, with specimens or photographs in support. We show a specimen, usually leaves or a small branch. They are immediately recognized by the healers. As a test, we have some specimens of the same species but with significant variation. But the healers are never confused; Diakité and Coulibaly always have a local name that corresponds with the western classification of species. They never disagree. Most species have many uses. Firewood. Building poles. Fodder. Utensils. Fiber. House supports. Food. Drinks. But most of all, medicines. Leaves for infusions for malaria. Barks for muscle pain. Flowers for infusions for diarrhea. Fruits for potency. Roots as aphrodisiacs. We joke that none of us needs that.

For some of the specimens, I can say the Bambara name and sometimes mention the uses I know from the literature.

When we get to specimen 43, I say the Bambara name for the species and list the uses I know. Diakité corrects my pronunciation but says:

"This stranger knows something about trees."

"My knowledge is small compared to yours," I say.

The healer paused for a moment. He points at my beard and then tugs his own. He says something that I don't quite catch, and I ask for a translation from Cissé.

"He says that the billy goat is not older than his owner."

I think for a moment, but I don't follow. Many Malian aphorisms are vague, almost Zen-like. There are often several meanings.

Cissé continues: "You know how male goats have that little beard? Well, it means that just because you have a beard doesn't mean that you're more experienced than…."

"I get it," I say. "I get it."

In case I may have missed the point, Cissé adds, "And it seems like you're the buck and not the owner."

"I get it."

When we get to specimen 54, there is finally a short discussion between the healer and his apprentice. I ask Cissé what is happening. There is some doubt about a possible use, but Coulibaly says that when he was in Kita he saw a healer use the leaves in a tea for toothaches.

I am suspicious. Although the healers confirm many of the uses found in the literature, I begin to think that they invent uses to please us.

At 58, there is a slight hitch. Two closely related species of *Terminalia* cause a bit of a problem. Western science knows these as two separate species. But for Diakité and Coulibaly they are male and female versions of the same species. In Western botany, there are tree species that present female and male trees. The Gingko is a well-known example. But I double-check. These are, in fact, separate species. But all in all, this strikes me as a minor difference in the understanding of botany.

We are almost through the list and every species has a use, most have 3 or 4. I am skeptical. How can each species have a use? Why aren't there any useless trees, trees that just exist, or trees that are considered "weeds"?

I ask Cissé if they are not making up uses. He swears they are not. He says that perhaps no one person knows all the uses for a tree, but someone else will know.

I remain skeptical. It doesn't seem logical to me, it doesn't seem rational, that all species have a use.

I push back on Diakité.

"Surely there must be a tree or a plant that isn't useful. Just some random tree?" I ask.

Diakité rubs his beard and looks at me.

"Young brother," he says patiently, almost as if to someone who has lots of information but little knowledge, "why would God create a tree without a purpose?"

THE MARABOUT

We are in the right neighborhood but not sure of where to turn. A phone conversation in Wolof between the taxi driver and an unknown person ensues. Fatima says the marabout is young. She clearly thinks, correctly, that I have another preconception. We turn down a sandy side street and stop. We wait. We see a strange dog on the street—I wonder aloud that maybe it has a tumor or a broken hind leg. Fatima says, "Why don't you ask?"

We see a man waving from down the street. Fatima says, "There he is."

We shake hands as we are ushered into the hallway of the compound. We can't go into the main room of the house because it is already occupied by clients of the marabout. We continue down the hallway and enter a bedroom. There is a large bed taking up most of the space, cluttered night tables, and an armoire. The marabout brings in a plastic chair for me. Fatima and the marabout perch on the bed.

We chat a little bit, with Fatima translating. Then we get down to business. The marabout asks why I have come. I say that I think that God has given me capabilities and talents, but that I don't seem to always use them well. I want to be able to give the best that I have. He asks why I don't think I am reaching my potential. I say that sometimes I am scared to take risks. I say that sometimes I worry too much about what other people think. Fatima interrupts her translating to look at me and say, "That's everybody."

The marabout asks my name. He asks me to write it out. Apparently, Fatima knows my handwriting already and takes the paper and writes it down. She shows me—"That's it, right?" She gives it to the marabout, who leaves and comes back after a minute with a well-used, handwritten booklet. The script is Arabic. He borrows Fatima's phone, with the familiar red case, and using the calculator function, runs through several computations. Once he gets a figure, he rifles through the dog-eared pamphlet and reads silently. Apparently, my name corresponds to certain numbers put together in certain ways. Their interaction provides a view of what is happening beneath the surface and in the future. Finally, he says not to worry—that I have not been bewitched or put under a spell. I think I am supposed to feel relieved. He says it's just the normal "evil eye" and "bad mouthing."

I almost push the point and say that I am not worried about the evil eye or bad mouthing. I am more worried about the enemy within. But I sense that this is not a common theme for the marabout. Unless, somehow, that is what this process of externalization is for—for us to be more aware of personal weaknesses.

He provides his prescription. It includes sacrificing a goat or sheep, giving away the meat, taking a certain part and making a *gris-gris*—a ring or a leather pouch. It also includes the preparation of special water with writing from the Koran that I am to bathe with.

He points out that I do not have to decide right away—I can think about it. I say okay.

Apparently, this initial consultation costs $2. This seems cheap for mental health care. I give him $10. Everyone seems happy. We leave past kids ricocheting in the hallway and women doing domestic chores, slowed by Fatima's chatting with everyone.

THE WOMAN AND THE WRITER

The woman first appears in the short story "All That" published by Granta in 2003. There she is Sarah Burnhart. In the story, Sarah is a bright young woman who, after a Master's degree in international affairs, goes overseas to work with the UN refugee organization in Sudan. The story worked well, especially the part of Sarah.

The writer, Frank Beerman, lives alone in an old wooden house in Loudon County outside Washington, D.C. He is a frequent contributor to Gargoyle and the Appalachian Review. He becomes engrossed in developing Sarah's life and looks. The way she smiles. Her walk. The birthmark on the side of her neck. The way she often would say, "I'll say." The way she tilts her head. Her clothes—often jeans, running shoes, and t-shirts when she isn't working. She is slim and athletic and smart.

When Beerman meets other women, he starts, almost unconsciously, to compare them to the woman he now calls Sarah. Often, they don't seem as charming. They do not smile enough or in the right way. They do not have the perfect response. They have strange laughs. Their clothes are not casually enticing. They do unexpected things. Often, these things ruin the tone or tempo of the situation, something Sarah would never do—at least not after several rewrites.

Beerman writes two other stories with women characters. One is published by Black Lagoon and the other by the Writers' Cooperative. The women in these stories are different from Sarah, yet they seem to have many of Sarah's characteristics.

In 2005, he writes a story called "I hear what you're saying." In that story, there is also a woman who had many of the characteristics of Sarah. He begins to realize that all his main women characters are versions of Sarah. If they are blonde, it is because Sarah has dyed her hair. If they are tall, Sarah had on heels. If they are mean, it is because Sarah is good at pretending to be mean.

The writer grows increasingly preoccupied with Sarah. He likes the way he could make her do things. Play different roles. Wear different clothes. He begins to write short descriptions of Sarah and himself in different situations. Not for publication. She always treats him the way he wants to be treated. Frankly, she can be submissive.

He publishes two other stories, and the women characters are always Sarah acting out different roles. He begins to worry that he can't create a new woman character at all, that all his women characters are Sarah. He worries that his critics, of whom there are many, will point out the fact that his imagination is limited. That he only created and understood one character. That wigs and makeup do not truly create other characters. All his characters are poor variations on a single perspective and viewpoint. He fears the day when they will discover that he is a fraud, a limited writer, with no fundamentally new insights into women characters.

He begins to become somewhat protective of the woman. And jealous also. When he is not writing about her and rereading his stories about her, he wonders what she is doing. He feels sometimes that she might be involved with other writers' stories. That they might make her do things that were not good. Or that she might enjoy being in those other stories, that she might be more beautiful and the situations more interesting and meaningful than his stories. That they might make her do things that would turn her against him.

He puts a portable bed and a small refrigerator in his attic. When he is not writing about the woman, he locks her there. Still, he wonders if this is effective. He reads another writer's story and he is sure that the woman with the pet dog is Sarah. The other writer used makeup and high collars, but he could still see the faint birthmark on her neck. In another story, she is an older woman who has a stroke while getting off a bus with her son. She really did a good job in that story, transforming herself into a conflicted older woman. It is amazing.

It feels a bit perverse, but he continues to lock her in the attic. He hopes that people can't find her and will not be able to find out he is a fraud. She does not like being confined. They have their first argument. She shouts at him. She begins to be stubborn and withdrawn.

His next story, called "I'll say," gets rejected by four magazines. One editor tells him that the characters are no longer compelling. Critics lambast his portrayal of women as one-dimensional and repetitive. An article in the New York Review of Books is particularly vicious.

The woman finds several boxes of novels and short story collections in the attic and begins to spend hours reading. She also finds several half-used notebooks and pens in the attic. She begins to write. She writes for four hours a day when she is not reading or involved with the writer. She writes several short stories. Several of these are about a writer who has lost his touch. In her stories, the writer becomes obsessive. He becomes distracted and forgetful. He loses touch with reality.

One day, when the writer visits Sarah in the attic, he discovers that she is not there. He searches everywhere. Somehow, she has left. He wonders if he should call the police, but he knows that that will raise too many questions.

He begins to feel that he can no longer control his life and his impulses. He finds himself doing strange things, like driving too fast or using drugs. At a bar, he meets a woman who is very beautiful and very strong-willed. He has too much to drink and goes home with the woman. In the morning, he finds that she has thrown his old clothes away and bought him new clothes. To please the woman, he finds he continues to do things that are out of character. He buys her flowers. They plan a trip to Paris together. She gets him to stop swearing.

The writer first appears as Frank Beerman in the short story "The Woman and the Writer" by a new writer named S. Burnhart, published by The Vermont Review in the fall issue in 2016.

TYRONE

As we approach Tyrone, we see in the great distance a large structure silhouetted against the sky, looming on the horizon. It is so large; it dwarfs a nearby water tower. It is boxy and must be man-made. It is taller than any bell tower, spire, or minaret. It confuses us. It is so huge and so ominous that it makes me slightly anxious. We try to figure out what it is—some huge factory? Some large military installation? As we get closer and it comes more completely into view, we abruptly realize that it is the Penn State football stadium.

I say, "Look at the size of that thing. Jesus."

"No…," she says. "Paterno."

We wind through Tyrone to the place we were staying. The central part of the main street, Pennsylvania Avenue, is only a couple of blocks long—with run-down houses on small lots, a Burger King, a community pharmacy, a liquor store, Paul's Amoco, Nino's Italian restaurant. At the liquor store, I get a bottle of Martini and Rossi extra-dry vermouth. On a side street, a girl in t-shirt and jeans is practicing with a baton, sending it into long arcs in the air. She intently watches it as a boy on a stoop, just as intently, watches her.

We stopped to let a small group of people cross the road. Two women and three kids, tow-headed kids with fishing poles. The women are smoking.

Turning up the hill, a car is stopped in the middle of the road. We wait. An old man shuffles out of the door and across the porch of a worn house. He is hurrying very slowly. One by one he takes the steps and slowly comes out on the street. Instead of getting in the car, he crosses the street. A younger man finally comes out and, without acknowledging us, gets in the car and drives off.

We stay at the Stony Haven Bed and Breakfast, a large stone house with Masonic symbols and huge rooms. On the TV is an old black-and-white movie with Clark Gable and Claudette Colbert, *It Happened One Night*. The house and the movie reminded me of my mom. The owner of the B&B is in his forties and used to work with an ad agency in Philadelphia. He is here because of a "mid-life crisis." He looks hard at me. "You know what I mean," he says.

In the morning, we find we have a flat tire. The car only has a temporary spare—not an extra tire. I try to take the flat off but after jacking the car and removing the lug nuts, the tire seems soldered to the car. We call roadside assistance and after two hours, a guy shows up. He also has trouble getting the tire off, finally whacking it with an old section of a 4 by 4. We are forced to be patient, to wait.

At the Breyer School near the cemetery, an old woman shows us into the library with old yearbooks. We find the one with my mom. The old woman leaves us in the reading room. I stare at the full-page photo of my mom, an intimate stranger. She looks old and young; familiar and foreign. I had never seen my mom as she appeared in the yearbook. She was tall and thin, with a hint of mischief. She was ready for the world. Inexplicably, her nickname is "Beabsy." I had never heard anyone call her that. She was athletic. She was involved in music. Under her picture was an amateur sonnet referring to a distant love. It was not written by her. It is not about my father. Dimensions of her that I never knew.

My wife touches the back of my neck. The yearbook makes a "thunk" as we close it. The old woman thanks us for stopping by. At the gate, there are piles of leaves.

The cemetery was along a winding road that ran between a small river and the hills. We passed a water treatment plant and a rock pit. The cemetery was in the small town of Birmingham, a square of houses at the foot of the hills.

There is a large white wooden, austere building on the cemetery grounds. It looks like it could be a church, but it has no spire or cross. High up are stained glass windows; some sections have been replaced with plywood. A large maple tree has lifted and cracked the concrete steps in front. A plaque says it is the Laura Green Memorial Lounge. I wonder about lounging here. The door is padlocked.

We park and wander among the graves until we get to the Sullivan section. Mom is there, a simple flat headstone at the edge of the cemetery. She is almost under the large hedgerow that forms the border between the cemetery and the dirt road. Because of the overhanging branches, it is impossible to stand directly in front of her grave. She is at the edge, the fringe. And she will be here forever.

We open the bottle of vermouth. The smell brings back a flood of memories of my mom in the kitchen cooking while we sat around doing homework. Her damp hands. The memory is as fresh as it was a quarter of a century ago. When I am gone, no one will miss it, no one will remember it.

I say, "Here's to you, Mom," and take a drink from the bottle. I pass it to my wife who takes a drink. We pour a little on the grave. I take another drink.

"Well," I say to the grave, "we miss you a lot. We think about you every day. You were a great mom. We learned a lot from you. I'm sorry you are stuck out here on the edge of the cemetery. I hope that we have lived up to your expectations of us. We are not always good people, but we are not totally bad either, I hope. Anyway, the Irish in you doesn't want too much dwelling on the past, I suppose."

I take another drink. "The Irish in you probably doesn't want us moping around either."

My wife says, "Careful, you're driving." I need to be careful since I am driving.

But her headstone is silent, waiting.

We drive out of Tyrone, through the boarded-up houses expectantly waiting destruction or revival.

Outside of town, we come upon a view of rows and rows of dark blue and gray hills. The dull serrations of the hills silently grating, grating against the overcast sky.

THE DISTANCE BETWEEN

Initially, the distance between us was about 3 feet. That's how wide the tables are in the booths at Trio's. That was the first six months or so.

After that, the distance became less until one night, the distance was zero. Then, at night, it often was zero. Sometimes it became so close that it was slightly negative.

Then one day it went back to three feet.

She said, "The distance between two people is always infinite."

I said, "Ok. So? If it's everyone then why can't it be us?"

She got up. I watched her retreat. At the door, she punched her arms through her jacket and put on her pack. She hiked it up. She went through the door and out of sight.

The distance seemed infinite.

Like the distance between here and

JUST A SHOT AWAY

I recognized him immediately. The beard, longer hair, and baggy clothes did not obscure the eyes and the sloping shoulders. We hugged in the doorway for a moment while I tried to keep the dogs from knocking him over.

Sara came into the living room and I introduced them: Scot, Sara; Sara, Scot. They shook hands. She said that she had heard a lot about him. She excused herself to go help the kids pack for camp.

We sat across from each other. He had his hands on the dogs' heads, scratching behind their ears.

"Who are these guys?" he asked.

"The black one is O'Connor and the yellow one is O. Henry. If you want them both just say O."

"Oh." he said and the two dogs stopped panting, cocked their heads and stared expectantly at him.

"How long has it been? It must be 20 years. Since high school," I said.

"Yes," he said, "20 years to the day."

"It was graduation night, I think."

"Yes. That's why I'm here."

He reached to get something out of the inside pocket of his green army jacket. Under his left arm was a rich, dark brown, leather holster, polished with age and use. The stitching of the seams was still perfect. Jutting out was the black and silver handle of a revolver. He paused. I looked at his face and thought I saw a brief grin, but if it was ever there, it was gone. He was solemn, serious. He continued to reach into his pocket and pulled out a folded, worn piece of paper. He unfolded it deliberately. He glanced at it and then handed it to me.

It was in my handwriting and it was signed by me. It was dated June 17, 1970. It read:

> "I, William Flannery, being of sound mind and body, hereby authorize and request that any of the following people: John Cheever, Scot Thomas, or Chris Andersen; to kill me if in 20 years I end up with a wife and two kids, living in the suburbs, with a 9 to 5 job and a two-car garage. Through the present, I absolve them of all criminal pursuit by such action and waive all rights of prosecution."

I tried to laugh. I felt the blood rush to my face. He took the paper back.

"We were crazy and naïve then. We had no idea about life," I said.

"We were crazy and naïve then?" he replied. "Why would you say that? It was real to us then—as real as this moment is now."

"No," I said, "we were young; we had no experience."

"No moment is superior to another," he said. "We make commitments. Sometimes we keep them. Sometimes we don't."

"This is crazy," I said. "This can't be why you are here. That isn't a legal document." As soon as I said it, I knew it sounded stupid.

Very slowly and deliberately, he said, "Do I look like I am here on behalf of law enforcement or the judicial system? There are larger forces. We need to talk. But not in front of the family. Let's go for a drive. It won't take long."

I called out to Sara that we were going out for a beer.

As we left the house, I did not see an unfamiliar car parked nearby. He asked me to drive my car. He told me to go to West Rock. Sitting in the front passenger seat, he pulled a silencer out of his pants pocket and withdrew the revolver from its holster. With care and precision, he screwed the silencer on to the revolver and laid the revolver in his lap. He asked me to take Spring Street.

I broke the silence. "You know when I wrote that, it was graduation, a lot of things going on, maybe we were high."

He said, "Only a coward would denigrate himself and that moment."

After that, aside from him giving directions, we did not talk.

After the graduation ceremony, we had all piled into Chris's car and driven out to the beach. By the time we got there, it must have been midnight or later. We lugged a case of beer across the dunes to the surf. The four of us stood, barefoot, the waves coasting up to our ankles, looking out over the ocean, drinking. It was very dark. There was a summer lightning storm in the distance, on the horizon.

"That's moving east," said Chris.

Every once in a while, the flashes of light would reveal sheets of rain and the silhouette of a ship in the distance. The ocean seemed so deep and empty, inspiring and menacing at the same time. We knew that graduation was a turning point for us. I was anxious and hopeful for the future. As we stood looking out into the darkness, we began to talk about what futures we wanted for ourselves. It was about doing things that were important, different, exciting. It was about a break with our past.

> "I will not become my father," I shouted. "I will not settle. I will not die a death from a thousand cuts. I will do something, go somewhere. I refuse to be a nine-to-fiver. I will have a thousand friends, and they will glow like hot coals."

There was a pause.

Then Chris shouted, "I will not be that frog."

There was a moment of silence, then a deep burst of laughter.

> "Not be that frog? What the hell are you talking about?"
> "You know. Mr. Barley's biology class."
> "Un huh," a skeptical chorus.
> "Yeah. You know, *the frog*. If you put a frog in hot water, it jumps out. But if you put the frog in a pot and slowly raise the temperature, it will boil before it jumps out. It never notices. Don't be that frog."
> "Don't be that frog!" We all shouted into the empty ocean. "I will not be that frog!"

On the way back to town, I found a paper and pen in Chris's glove compartment and, with a lot of help on the wording, I had written out the agreement. I signed it. The three of them voted that Scot should keep it. He folded it and put it in his wallet. Back in town, we split up, each seeking our luck in the world. I had not seen Scot again. Chris and John I had seen a few times.

We turned off at the entrance to the West Rock Park and started up the hill. About a quarter mile up, we came to a set of orange traffic cones and a wooden barricade. There was a green pick-up parked slightly off the road. He told me to move the barricade and go through. I stopped after the barricade and replaced it.

"No witnesses," he said enigmatically.

We continued up the winding road to the lookout, and I parked across from a bench. New Haven spread out before us, the regular grid of the roads lit up by streetlights and the occasional car. It continued out to a small set of hills in the distance. It was slightly cooler here with a breeze. The crickets kept a low buzz. A three-quarter moon gave everything a glow.

There was a summer thunderstorm brewing in the distance. He said it was coming this way.

He asked me to sit on a stone wall facing the view while he sat on the bench behind me with the revolver on his lap. He took a small cassette recorder from his jacket and put a tape on. It was the Stones' "Gimme Shelter." It took me back to our last year in high school. Chris, Scot, John, and I listened to the album all the time that year.

The constant refrain came on…

"It's just a shot away, shot away, shot away."

"Ok," he said "Talk to me."

"What do you mean?"

"Stop the bullshit," he said. "You made a commitment on this day in 1970. As far as I can tell you have a wife and two kids, you live in the suburbs with a two-car garage; you have a 9-to-5 job. Tell me what happened. Start on June 17th, 1970."

I started to talk. About going off to college that fall. About feeling lost most of the time. About finding a few good friends and mentors. About meeting Sara and falling in love. About economic concerns and getting a job. About having kids. About choosing a house and place to live. Some things just seemed to have happened without much thought. Like a branch floating in a stream. Other things I had always agonized about. In all appearances, I had ended up like my father, but with better technology.

I realized that the cassette was on a loop—playing "Gimme Shelter" over and over.

There had been a lot of small decisions. A lot of missed opportunities. A lot of unintended consequences. A lot of just getting by and taking the easy road. This was all true. But can't there be joy and accomplishment in the little moments? Can't we, as imperfect humans, flooded with misunderstood feelings, scrap together a decent life with all its warts and stupidities?

Finally, I stopped talking. The wind had picked up and the leaves of the trees showed their undersides. I don't know how long I talked, but I completed a history of sorts up to that night. I sat there silently. It began to drizzle and then to rain heavily. I knew he was no longer there.

I sat until I thought I had enough strength and energy to get up. I stood, taking a small step to catch myself, and looked out at the regular pattern of the town. I turned and walked back to the car in the rain, picking up the cassette player as I went. By the time I got to the car, I was soaked. I took a couple of deep breaths. I drove slowly down the mountain. The barricade and the truck were gone.

The visibility became bad as I left the park and joined the main road. I pulled over and waited. I wiped my eyes. After a while, I let out a guffaw of relief and pounded the steering wheel. All I could hear crashing over and over in my head was:

"Love, sister, it's just a kiss away, kiss away, kiss away."

The rain made the town glitter. The streetlights stood like sentinels. The large windows of the houses radiated a welcome to come in out of the rain and dark. There seemed to be hundreds of these new glowing openings, invitations at every turn.

I parked on the street since the garage was so full of junk only Sara's car could fit. It was raining heavily. I ran to the door and got in as fast as I could. O. Henry and O'Connor met me at the door. They stared expectantly past me to see if someone else was there. I was soaked and went straight to the laundry room and took off my clothes. I took a shower and put on clean, dry clothes.

I went downstairs to the TV room to see Sara. The dogs were on the couch on either side of her like bookends. They were more jealous than usual. I had to squeeze in, to sit next to Sara. I put my arm around her. She briefly tilted her head so her ear touched by shoulder. I think the news was on.

"How was it?" she said.

"Not everyone has friends like I do."

"What did you talk about?"

"Frogs," I said.

THE COUNTER

He didn't remember exactly when he began to count things. He first noticed it when he was brushing his teeth. Ten times on the right side, ten times in front, ten times on the left side. Then again ten times on the tops and bottoms on each set of molars. Always the same order. Sometimes repeated twice or three times depending on how bad he felt. The worse he felt, the more he brushed; it gave him a sense of order.

Then he noticed he was also counting the number of times he stirred his coffee. Always exactly 12 times. Clockwise. If he went over 12, he dumped the coffee out and started again.

Around the time she left him, he started counting the number of steps on his walk to the subway station. At first, it varied somewhat. But eventually he grew to target a certain number—1,016. He got so he knew it exactly and he always wanted it to be the same. If he was getting closer and the steps were already high, he would lengthen his stride to make it exactly 1,016. If he was close and the number was low, he would start to take smaller steps.

He began to count everything. He realized that most things were not only countable but actually made to be counted. Counting had a beginning and an end. It was predictable. It helped him feel in control, especially after she left him.

He counted the offices in the hall on the way to his own office.

He counted telephone poles on sections of his commute. He counted the number of people in his subway car. It began to amaze him that some people took the metro for years and never once knew exactly how many people were in their metro car.

There were some things that cried out to be counted. Jumping jacks. Stairs. Stairs were invented for counting more than for getting up and down.

He counted the seconds it took for the coffee maker to turn off. He counted the minutes it took to defrost a 1-pound package of ground beef. He counted the windows on the office across the street. He counted the number of passenger trains that passed on the tracks that he could barely see from the office window. He counted the seconds it took for him to urinate. He counted the number of words in articles in the newspaper.

It began to affect him at work. To others, he appeared distracted, but they did not realize that he was committed to counting the number of meetings, the number of minutes in each meeting, the number of emails, the number of lines in an email. They didn't realize how important this work was.

His colleagues at work began to consider him absent-minded. They called him into a meeting. They talked about his performance and that it wasn't the first time. How, he thought, could they talk about his performance when they did not even know how many chairs were in the room, or how many windows were in the office? He bet most of them did not even know how many steps it took them to get home. Or the number of strokes in brushing their teeth.

Eventually they asked him to leave.

On his way home he counted the telephone poles along certain sections of the metro line. He counted the 1,016 steps home from the station. He counted the seconds it took for the coffee maker to turn off. He counted the number of times he stirred his coffee. He counted the number of times he brushed his teeth.

He put on his pajamas with the three buttons down the front. He got into bed. He lay on his back with his arms to his sides. He closed his eyes. He started to count the number of seconds.

ROSEMARY

Rosemary believed she had lived before, and in Italy. Or maybe the south of France. Definitely somewhere where they produced and consumed a lot of wine. Which, at this point, she felt she needed a few dozen more glasses.

A man gets up. A man sits down.

Okay looking. Has a job. Check. Nonsmoker. Check. Likes cats. Strike three. Cats. Ever since her friend recommended to her that she visit Keats' grave in Rome, she hated cats. The cemetery was crawling with them. Old ladies putting out scraps for them everywhere. Who knew cats liked pasta? Christ, it was like an enormous litter box. She thought maybe it was some weird Catholic ritual. The whole place smelled like cat urine. If she had another incarnation in Italy, it definitely wasn't in Rome.

A man gets up. A man sits down.

A beard. A sporty type. Bingo. Likes hiking. Uncheck. No more hiking for Rosemary ever since that incident at Bear Mountain. There they were hiking along when a huge bear leaped out onto the path and beat its chest. Everyone almost had a heart attack. Turned out it was only that asshole Jack in a bear suit. Jesus. Who gets dressed up in a bear suit to scare people?

A man gets up. A man sits down.

Older gentleman. Nonsmoker. Check. Likes to travel. Check. All he remembers from his trip to India is an accident he witnessed between a rickshaw and a police vehicle. Uncheck.

A man gets up. A man sits down.

Has job. Check. Brags about job. Uncheck. Brags about everything. Strike four. What is he, 12? By the end of the time, Rosemary feels like tearing her clothes, digging a hole, and burying herself.

A man gets up. A man sits down.

Well-built. Short hair. Neat.

"I am not with law enforcement," he says.

"You get that a lot?"

"You would not believe."

"Good or bad?"

"Some women dig the gun and uniform thing, but most don't. So I like to be clear."

Silence.

Finally, he says, "What are you doing here?"

"The same thing you are."

"Are you sure? Are you sure you are not here just going through the motions? So that you can go home and say to yourself you tried?"

"I'm more optimistic than that."

"Really? Do you know how many hours there are in a lifetime? And you are spending two of them here just going through the motions. There are so many other things you could be doing."

"You too."

"What I mean is, is this the best way toward your goal?"

"It's fairly direct, yes."

"But I don't know. What if you were doing something more useful?"

"Like what?"

"Volunteering at the hospital. Cleaning a river. Tutoring kids. You name it?"

"I'm not Mother Teresa."

"No, you're not. Does that mean you can't do these things?"

"Why are you on my case. You sound pretty preachy. Superior. Are you sure you don't have weaknesses?"

He paused. Then he says, "I fart a lot. A lot."

A man gets up. Another man sits down.

A man gets up. Another man sits down.

A man gets up. A man sits down.

Someone says, "Time's up" and "Thank you very much." She thinks: finally.

Rosemary walks home from the bus stop. As usual, she stops and gets a pint of Ben & Jerry's Chocolate Chocolate Chip and a People magazine. But unlike her usual routine, she puts the ice cream in the freezer, the magazine on the table, and begins to clean the kitchen. When it is orderly, she goes and gets ready for bed. Brushing her teeth, she looks at herself in the mirror. She does not like what she sees.

Lying in bed she thinks about the man. She wonders if she had met him before, in another life? Maybe another life, another incarnation, can tell her what to do, how to act?

She attempts, as she always does, to say to herself she tried. Usually it works. Tonight though, she thinks, "Uncheck."

THE GREEN STATION WAGON

Even after all these years, there were some noises—luckily not very common—that would cause him to panic intensely. It was mostly grating sounds, mostly metallic. It filled him with a flashing and uncontrollable sense of dread, emptiness. Of guilt and of loss—as if nothing would ever be the same. They passed quickly when he discovered what the noise actually was—a fork on a plate in a restaurant, or maybe a rake on concrete.

He has not been back to Sayville and the south shore of Long Island in almost 40 years. At the *Long Island Advance* offices, he asks whether they have back issues from 1971. A gruff older woman directs him to a tiny room with microfiche and a microfiche reader. He searches through news stories for the month of August. He finds it more quickly than he anticipated—an article from the August 23 edition, second page, lower right-hand corner. A picture of an overturned vehicle. A story about the crash on Montauk Highway that took the lives of a father and his two young sons.

He also has unwelcome visions from time to time. The abrupt swerve of the green station wagon and its flipping onto its passenger side and shrieking across the asphalt for

100 feet. The sparks shining brightly in the evening darkness. Once the car reaches the median, it begins to violently and unevenly roll several times. It ends up in the freshly cut grass surrounded by dust, its tires spinning in the air. The roof is entirely collapsed onto the body of the vehicle.

He knows the family name now—Wilson. And he perhaps now knows the address, if the wife and daughter have not moved. They are older now. Perhaps they have moved on. He checks the phone book. There is still a Maryann Wilson at the address.

The house is a solid house in an older neighborhood. It is white. There is a large tree in the yard. The walkway is brick with short, stubborn weeds here and there. He stands before the door. He breathes slowly. He knocks at the door. A woman comes and opens it partially.

"I would like to talk to you about a car crash on August 22, 1971."

The woman hesitates and then says, "Come in."

He sits as indicated in the simple living room. There are several old photos of a man and two small boys on the end tables.

"Yes?" she says.

He inhales and starts. "I was 17. I was hitchhiking along Montauk Highway going out East to see my girlfriend. It was the evening of August 22. Near the exit for Shirley, a man stopped to pick me up. He just stopped in the middle of the road. He was drunk. A green station wagon came up behind us, and the driver had to swerve to avoid us. The drunk never noticed, but I saw the crash. We drove away."

A SERVANT OF PEACE

I slapped him hard across the face.

"Snap out of it, man," I said. "We have to figure out how to disarm this nuclear bomb!"

He slapped me back. Hard.

"I'm snapped out of it already! I think maybe it's only a clock," he said, "and not even an electronic one, it's like a wind up!"

"What do you know? Do you even have an undergraduate degree in rocket science or horology or a related field, or ten years of relevant experience?" I said, rubbing my jowls and squinting through my hairy eyebrows, using my pale blue eyes the color of coffee grounds.

"Does satellite imagery count?"

"Yes."

"Too bad I don't have that either. But I use the internet."

My good friend Robin was always a little slow on the uptake. How could he not mistake the loud ticking for the presence of plutonium? And the men we had seen in the neighborhood did not seem to be horologists; judging by their white coats and mustaches, they must have been intent on being disguised as urologists. Confusing the two was a common mistake and one my friend made all too frequently.

"Hello, boys," came a voice behind us. "Maybe I can help?"

I whirled around. "Batgirl!" I exclaimed.

"No, there is no Batgirl. You're thinking Catwoman," said Robin. He smirked.

"There is so a Batgirl. As any nitwit knows."

"Catgirl," I continued, "we have to disarm this nuclear bomb. It's ticking louder now, which leads me to believe that we have to act fast or that the wind has changed direction. Perhaps the humidity has gone down, allowing for sound waves to propagate…"

"Catwomyn, " she said coolly. "It's Catwomyn. M-Y-N."

"Is that like a plural? I mean like, are there more than just you?" said Robin. He was clearly hoping that there were lots more. He was king of embarrassing questions.

"Enough," I said. "We have to act quickly. If not, all of Rubbleton will be reduced to …" I hated to think.

If this were a ten-megaton device, as I suspected, its detonation would, depending on the wind direction and speed and relative humidity, greatly diminish cell phone reception over a wide area for the next several weeks at least. Especially for those who weren't on the AT&T family plan. And the impact on global warming could be on the order of magnitude of 0.8 to 0.83 degrees over the next 30 years, especially within a 2-yard radius of the denotation.

I looked at the human resources available to me. There was Robin. Energetic but sadly unfamiliar with nuclear devices, horology, or women. His constant chirping was also very annoying. Then there was whoever it was that claimed to be this mysterious Catwomyn. Was she an ally or one of them?

"Do you know the difference between horology and urology?" I demanded.

"Who wants to know?"

I had to think about that one. I mean do we really, really ever know who we are? Can we ever really trust our own judgments? Maybe it all comes down to whether we know how to disarm this nuclear warhead, which is sitting on our lawn, dropped off by one of those roving gangs of urologists.

"Never mind that," I said. "I'm just some poor sap, out to make just this little corner of the world a better place. Just a regular guy not wanting any thanks; just doing good and slipping back into the shadows. Just a servant of peace. Just a fighter against injustice."

"Oh, really?" she said.

I sensed her arching her eyebrows behind the cat mask. I was beginning to suspect that both Catwomyn and Robin were not as they appeared.

Down the street, a gang of urologists was sneaking behind a house.

NOTE FROM THE CAT-SITTER

appreciate you stopping in from time to time this weekend to check on my cat, make sure his water is filled and he has his food, and that the litterbox doesn't become too gross. Thanks.

No problem—here are my notes:

Saturday morning, 9:00 a.m. Found cat looking out window, sulking. Tried to cheer up cat. Cat has abandonment issues. I said you'd be back, but cat just keeps repeating "This isn't the first time. This isn't the first time, you know. That whore!" Cat showed me valium stash. Said he normally gets one. Clearly lying. Gave him half. He seems to chill a bit. The other two and a half I have included as part of my compensation package due to unforeseen circumstances.

Saturday noon. Caught cat smoking a doobie in the bathroom without the fan on. Severely chastised cat. Bad cat. Very BAD cat. Told cat repeatedly that having fan on was fundamental. Cat said something about a "lecture." Unfortunately, cat fails to see this as a learning opportunity. Confiscated cat's stash. Cat became angry. Stormed out of bathroom. Cat has anger management issues.

Saturday, 2:00 p.m. Cat lunges at me from behind the front door. Please find attached receipts for 1) outpatient services, 27 stitches $659, 2) carpet cleaning $250, and 3) cat declawing $200.

Saturday afternoon, 4:00 p.m. Brought back half of cat's stash. Smoked a couple of reefers. Cat offered bag of Doritos. Since a resident of the apartment offered the Doritos I do not feel I have to reimburse for them. Cat asked me if I have girlfriend. Cat says I should bring girlfriend over. I said I thought you were kinda cute. Cat can't stop laughing.

Sunday morning, 2:00 a.m. Surprise visit! Found apartment totally dark except for a few candles. Sade playing on the stereo. A bottle of wine and two glasses on the table. Cat comes racing out of bedroom totally naked. Immediately says that nothing is going on. I say, "Did I say something was going on?" He says, "No, but you were." I say, "But I didn't." He says, "No, but you were." I say, "But I didn't." He says, "No, but you were." I say, "But I didn't." Fifteen minutes later, I search apartment but find nothing, but while in bedroom hear whispering and front door close. Cat seems somehow resentful of my presence. Since wine was open, we decide to finish bottle. Cat drank at least half, if not more, frankly.

Sunday morning 9:00 a.m. Discover that I accidently did not leave apartment that night.

Sunday morning, 9:30 a.m. Cat going to town licking himself. Starts to choke. Points at throat. I perform Heimlich maneuver. Ginormous hairball emerges. Gi Nor Mous! In baggie in the fridge. Recommend submitting to Guinness.

Sunday afternoon. Watch football with cat. Cat's team is winning. Cat is frankly an unbearable, superficial, arrogant, little snot. Cat orders pizza then refuses to pay. Not even the tip. Luckily, I found where you keep your emergency fund.

Sunday evening. Last check in! Cat is sulking again. Asks how much I'm getting paid. I say it's just a favor, maybe a bottle of wine or a date. Cat is insulted. Calls you a cheapskate. Calls me a two-dollar whore. I leave.

Recommend counseling for cat.

BONE STEW

I t was number 175 or 176, she thought. She'd check when she got home. This one was a woman's, an older lady who had fallen. She didn't get as many of those. If it were a good one, she'd use it for a cane knob. If not, she'd give it to Frankie. She wondered if Frankie could tell the difference.

She was anxious to get to 200. Maybe she'd quit then. The stress of hospital protocol and all that bureaucracy around "proper disposal of medical waste" was getting to her. At the same time, there was something titillating about it.

When she got home, she examined it a bit more closely and decided that it was definitely one for Frankie. It was number 176. Frankie had gotten the great majority of them, maybe 140, and seemed to look forward to them almost daily. As usual, as soon as Frankie smelled it, Frankie became animated and seemed very eager, whining and wagging, not only her tail, but her whole back end. They were her favorite treat. She wondered if Frankie would get arthritis herself. But as a black lab, Frankie was bound to get it anyway. Maybe she would be obliged to give Frankie a replacement. That would be ironic.

That Saturday morning, she took Frankie to Rock Creek Park. It was fairly empty, so she let Frankie off the leash. To her surprise, Frankie immediately bolted for the woods as if she caught the scent of something. She continued walking for a bit, slowly so Frankie could catch up. It took longer than she expected and she turned back.

Finally, Frankie came back out of the woods, proudly carrying a stick. The dog loped up to her, wagging her tail. She tried to take the stick from Frankie to throw it, but Frankie wouldn't let go. It was then she realized that it was not a stick but actually a bone. She finally wrestled it from Frankie and examined it. She immediately recognized it as a human femur. Looking more closely, she knew that it was from a young female.

She stood in shock and confusion for several minutes, wondering what to do.

Finally, she decided to try to find where Frankie had gotten the femur. Holding the bone, she went back the way Frankie had come out of the woods. She tried to communicate to Frankie to show her where the femur had come from, but Frankie was no Lassie. Frankie jumped up continually to try to snatch the bone back from her.

After about 45 minutes of stumbling around in the woods, she found the place where Frankie had dug. The hole was not deep—about 12 inches. With a stick, she pried around where the dog had dug. She stepped back and held her breathe. There were the full skeletal remains of a human. Out loud she said, "Holy shit. Holy motherfucking shit." Again she wondered what to do. She leashed Frankie and threw the femur back in the hole that Frankie had dug.

She walked back out to the path and called 911. The conversations were a blur. She waited for the police to show up. There were two of them, a patrol officer and a detective. She showed them where Frankie had dug up the bone. Soon, there was a small crowd. The forensic pathologist showed up. They carefully exhumed the remains—except for the femur that Frankie had pulled up, all of the skeleton was there. They placed the bones in a series of plastic bags.

The detective, Lynch, according to his tag, took her contact information and asked what she did. She said she was a surgeon at George Washington. Lynch said if they needed more information, they'd be in touch.

She followed the news online. They were able to reconstruct some of what had happened. There were traces of a jogging outfit and shoes. DNA tests revealed the identity was that of a young woman who had been missing for six months. There was still the unique necklace that the parents tearfully identified. However, no arrests were made, although three suspects were brought in for questioning.

Two weeks later, Lynch called and said that he wanted to come by and thank her for her help. They arranged for a visit on a Sunday morning.

They chatted for a while about the crime and the lack of closure.

"You have some dog, Dr. Brown," said Lynch, rubbing Frankie's ears. "We combed that area of the park with well-trained sniffer dogs and got nothing. Your dog seems to have a nose for this."

"Yeah," she said, "seems that way, I guess."

"By the way," Lynch asked, "what kind of surgery do you do?"

"Hip joint replacements—3 or 4 times a week."

After a while, Lynch finished his coffee. He said he had to go.

"Why don't you stay a bit?" said Dr. Brown. "I have a bone stew on the stove."

MY FATHER IS MOWING IN THE BACK

I pull into the familiar driveway. I hear the sound of the mower and walk around the side of the house. He is mowing, his hands evenly spread on the push bar, his eyes focused on the grass in front of the mower. His shoulders are set, his jaw muscles flexing underneath his thin beard. He goes to the end of the yard and turns. He sees me. He raises one pale hand, not much higher than his chest, palm out. He continues to mow.

I sit in the kitchen, on my stool, in my spot. I look across the table at a stove that I have never seen before. She has always standing there. But today I can see the burners; the chipped white coatings; the dials, the one on the far left missing; the oven with the dirty white dish towel on the door handle.

I get a beer from the bottom left of the fridge and turn on the game on the small kitchen TV. It is the fifth inning. I watch the game and listen to my father steadily going back and forth outside.

During the 7th inning stretch, I go back outside to see how he is doing. He is going back over the area that he has already mowed. He sees me and raises his hand. He continues to mow.

Shortly after the game ends, the sound of the mower stops. I breathe. When he does not come in, I go back outside. The mower is out of gas, but he pushes it in straight lines, back and forth. I take a step forward, but he raises his hand again and says, "I'm fine."

I go back in and watch him through the window. I wish he would come in and, like me, just cry.

WHERE DID YOU GO?

"Where did you go?" she asked.

On the moonless night, I went out along the western ramparts and whispered encouragement to the watchmen as I passed.

"Where did you go?" she asked.

I went down to *Taverne du Port* and stood silently in a corner and watched the sailors and whores desperately dancing and grinding.

"Where did you go?" she asked.

I drove out to a deserted part of the beach and took off all my clothes and shouted curses at the ocean.

"Where did you go?" she asked.

I went deep into the forest and lay down and covered myself with earth until I felt it devouring me.

"Where did you go?" she asked.

I broke into the church at night and urinated on the altar.

"Where did you go?" she asked.

I went down to *Trenchville*, Rue Mandela, behind the *Lanterne Rouge* and picked a fight with three drunks.

"Where did you go?" she asked.

I went to the cemetery where my mother is buried, felt her presence, knew it was a lie, and cried.

"Where did you go?" she asked.

I gathered up all my regrets like unwanted kittens, in a huge sack, added rocks, and I threw it off Humboldt's Bridge.

"Where did you go?" she asked.

I found her, bound her, and we had sex.

"Where did you go?" she asked.

I broke all the bottles in the world and slashed my wrists as many times as there are bottles in the world and when I got to heaven, I told god to fuck off.

"Where did you go?" she asked.

I went back to the *Lanterne Rouge* and had sex with two whores in the alley.

"Where did you go?" she asked.

I went to the edge of the universe and stood guard.

"Where did you go?" she asked.

I climbed a Mayan pyramid and was struck by lightning that was meant for someone else.

"Where did you go?" she asked.

"Nowhere. Just making sure the front door was locked," I said. "I'm here now."

THE WRINKLE

In the Sahel, which is part of Africa, they often underneath every stone outside the villag
village, and underneath every stone outsidne
another village. Not necessarily a villuckens
a village that exists full size in an ur village.
verse. The village under the sto chan your vil-
the stone is found. More o than in your vil-
and cows and chickens than in your village.
village where you e evil, and can fly, and do
and donkeys h
Maybe the u are under a stone behind
lage! M ave counterparts in this othe
lage worse version of. Probably sir
wn in the chain of villages. Yo
abitants of that village but you
too bad, really, when you thir

UNDER THE FRIDGE

in general, the terrain is dark and covered with dust and grime

piece of shrimp, mainly tail, desiccated

three shriveled-up peas

small part of an orange peel

small wad of paper, perhaps a receipt from *Babies R US*

another pea

piece of a fridge magnet with the letters CONG

small blue birthday candle, never lit

piece of a gummy, perhaps an edible

small pill, perhaps a Xanax

q-tip, soiled now at both ends

torn corner of a color photograph,
with a man's elbow

baby spoon still zip-tied securely to its
cardboard packaging,
a corner of the packaging dented

6 small shards of glass, 2 with traces of blood (Type O neg)

THE MOST COMMON PACKING MISTAKES TO AVOID

Things to take:

- Ticket
- Yellow card
- Passport
- T-shirts (throw out the black one with the hole)
- Both pairs of jeans
- Shoes – one running, one that can pass for working
- Undies
- Socks
- My speakers
- Your letters
- My letters to you (if I can find them)
- The small Indonesian hand-carved yoga sculpture, "Meditating Yogi" crushed man, I gave it to you but you never seemed to like it
- My meds

- My books
- The medium pot with the thick bottom
- The small fry pan
- Half the spoons and forks
- That time at Arches National Park in Utah
- The games
- The deck of cards
- That time on the deck of the place in Vermont
- 2 towels
- Ring
- Space in your feelings
- Take car keys
- Non-recyclable swept-up pieces in a plastic bag
- Take the pictures
- Hope, do not forget hope

Things to leave:

- House keys
- That argument at Montauk lighthouse
- That thing with Robert
- The arguing, the sulking, the digs, the neglect
- Leave the small nastiness
- Do not take the regrets and the anger and the feelings of wanting revenge
- Three-quarters of your heart

DOWN ON DAUFUSKIE ISLAND

They stood under a live oak, the tree decked with Spanish moss, waiting for the others of the tour group. It was cold but not freezing. The sky was overcast and the wind made it colder still. The others were in the plantation house—a large, squarish, white house with an impressive front porch. Just the two of them remained behind. Her quick smile and easy laugh were temporarily gone. She was the local tour guide, and he was a tourist, although he hated the term. It made him think of perverted types of voyeurism, of a passive/aggressive style of observation that turned human beings into zoo animals or objects under glass. Passersby on a bus, ogling but not engaged. In this case, maybe even getting a strange pleasure from someone else's suffering. He thought that some types of tourism bordered on the unethical.

They were on Daufuskie Island, a South Carolina sea island, one that still doesn't have a bridge connecting it to the mainland. The only access is by boat. The lack of access had made it an attractive spot for those seeking to avoid the long reach of the prevailing political system, including that which promoted slavery. This included Amerindians, pirates, other outlaws, and escaped or freed slaves, smugglers. In addition, its climate and disease profile made it so that slave owners and others avoided the place for several months of the year. Now, however, it was attracting interest from investors.

"How long has Daufuskie been inhabited?" he asked.

"The oldest artifacts found show that Daufuskie was inhabited as early as 7,000 years ago. The island was originally inhabited by the Yamacraw Indians or their ancestors, who apparently were known for their hunting and fishing. We do not know much about their agriculture."

"What happened to them?"

"As settlers and their slaves came, in the 1600s and 1700s, they were driven out. It seems that some of them were part of the Trail of Tears in 1830. Some may still exist, assimilated in other ethnic groups in Florida and elsewhere. The name "*daufuskie*" comes from them. It means tip of the feather."

"Ha! I thought it was for an early Polish settler. Like other Amerindian place names—the name remains but they are long gone—another thing that was stolen from them. Were they compensated?"

"What do you think? It's called the Trail of Tears for a reason."

There are millennia of unknown and unwritten history here, he thought, glanced over by a few words on a plaque. It seemed to assume that the Yamacraw had no history. That there were no wars, and ceremonies; no heroes and songs, no poetry, no great events, no great accomplishments, no art, no education… People who could be erased easily since there was so little to erase. History is for the powerful.

A moment later, she asked, "Why don't you go in?"

"I'm not sure," he responded. "Maybe because it seems to be some kind of implicit endorsement. A type of continued glorification of an extreme evil. Giving attention to it somehow seems to validate it. Something that deserves to be forgotten."

"But does it really deserve to be forgotten?"

"Well, not forgotten but resisted and prevented from happening again."

She adjusted her long braids so they were in front. She seemed slightly out of breath.

"Have you visited Auschwitz?" he asked.

"Nope. Savannah is as far as I've gotten."

"I visited Auschwitz. You can visit the Nazi commander's home. But you also visit the gas chambers, the detention halls, the housing, Block 11, the crematorium, the pits where people were held until they died… But here you visit the plantation owner's home in a big empty field, with a dock on the creek and a beautiful lane of old trees covered in Spanish moss. "

The wind picked up.

"Where is the slave housing?" he asked.

"Tore down."

"Where is the slave kitchen?"

"Tore down."

"Where are the 'whipping posts' and the holding pens?"

"Tore down."

"Where is the praise house?"

"Gone."

"Seems like an important part of history was torn down. Maybe the most important in human terms."

"Perhaps. But what happened here happened generations ago."

"Is it still happening?"

"Maybe. In other forms. In some of the 'gates and golf' communities people like to have the opportunity to come out but are quite so keen on islanders going in."

The Spanish moss dripped from the oaks like the beards of the hanged.

"To deal with history, you must understand it. You must learn it. You can't put your head in the sand."

Yes, but a true version of it, not a sanitized version developed to suit those in power, he thought. And through general education and not optional sanitized tourism that shied away from things that could offend. He went in.

Finally, the group came out of the slave owner's house. They were chatting and remarking on the beauty of the surroundings and the architecture of the house.

The guide beamed and said, "I hope you enjoyed your visit."

–o–o–o–o–o–

About an hour later on the tour, they visited a small museum. The guide gave a quick tour and set people loose in the gift and book shop. She went out and sat on a wooden bench. He joined her.

"I can't believe this island was once mainly plantations and was heavily logged. It looks so natural, so wooded," he said.

"It's hard to sit here and see and hear the history," she said. "Look around you. Is what you see pristine, untouched nature? The beautiful live oaks and Spanish moss? It looks pristine, doesn't it? We tend to think that we are seeing new things, things without history. But no, it's the result of history."

He shifted on the bench.

She continued, "There is no pristine nature—here or anywhere. Every place has history but we tend to ignore it."

"That's what I try to do. I try to show the history and the Gullah culture but like all human enterprises, it is subject to selective memory and warping. Now it's a question of interpretation. 'Until the lion tells the story, the hunter will always be the hero.'"

-o-o-o-o-o-

"Do you know about Gorée?" he asked.

"What's that?"

"It's a sea island off of Dakar in Senegal. There's a colonial building there that has 'the door of no return.' It was a staging area for slave traders—last prep before the journey across the Atlantic. Who knows, maybe one of your ancestors came through there."

"Maybe."

"Can I ask if you feel more African or more American?"

"I feel Gullah, with my own culture and ways of seeing."

He thought that Gullah culture is certainly something to be celebrated, but its origins are linked to deep sin and evil. It seemed born of a desire to escape some terrible things.

"Do you think you have to pay for the sins of your forefathers? 'Our fathers sinned, and are no more; and we bear their iniquities?'" he said.

"What happened here and more broadly can't be forgiven and should not be forgotten. We choose to remember the good things, the resilient things," she said.

She leaned back and closed her eyes.

The tourist thought, "How difficult is it to forget? Especially if powerful people feel threatened by these memories."

"Every shut eye ain't sleep," she said.

He looked at her in profile. He thought: This person is an extreme acrobat, balancing on a high wire, suspended high above the crowds. In this country, a mistake could mean death. Death awaits always. But an acrobat cannot take a break, she cannot. She is balancing every minute of every day with no respite. She dreams balancing. Black faces and white faces looking up at her waiting… And yet she never cracks and falls. She is balancing above death and smiling to the crowd. A true smile. And she is not alone.

The wind picked up and it grew colder.

HOVENWEEP JULY 19, 2020

I had gotten up while it was still dark. I couldn't sleep anyway, and drove out to Hovenweep National Monument. It's about 45 minutes from the town of Blanding where I was staying. I thought I was the first one there. I had my day pack; the loaded Ruger made it slightly heavier than usual. I started on the loop trail, which is well marked and well interpreted, and I had a map with short descriptions of the points of interest—mainly Amerindian ruins from around 1200. It is beautiful country, with low, sparse vegetation and stark sandstone formations. Much of the trail is over slickrock with only small cairns marking the way. There were a few puffs of clouds in the uncompromising sky. It was just getting light and warming up. As the earth warmed and stretched, a single loud clap reverberated down the canyon. Perhaps just the world cracking its knuckles.

At the first overlook, across the small canyon, there were a series of house-like ruins at the top of the canyon, in the canyon walls and on the talus slopes. The ruins were stone structures, some several stories tall, of elegant and refined masonry. Each flat sandstone slab keeping its unique shape and occupying a unique and customized slot in the building.

The structures have no edges and are built into and take advantage of the terrain. It is not always clear how one might enter or exit the buildings. Some seem to hang, suspended in the air, off the canyon rim. They were like corpses—empty shells without souls.

Across the canyon, I could see a seated figure in my spot, not very far from the ruins, under a small juniper tree. I thought it must be a fellow hiker who had a good view of the ruins and the head of the canyon that I was about to circumnavigate.

As I made my way around to the other side, a particular multi-story ruin came into view that was perched on the canyon floor. Called the Square Tower, it was the only structure with defined edges. But the edges are not straight; the entire structure has a slight purposeful twist to it. It is as if the weight and shape were helping to screw the tower into the ground. Or preparing it to leap toward the sky.

It took me about an hour to get around to the other side. The man was still there in his spot, contemplating the view. He was not far off the trail and I approached. I walked slowly to where the man sat, looking at the early morning sun traversing the landscape and highlighting the ruins across the canyon.

"A beautiful sight," I said.

The figure was silent.

"A good spot," I said.

I said, "Lost in thought."

He didn't reply. He was young—maybe in his twenties with blonde hair, now tinged with red. He was dressed in jeans and a t-shirt. He was limp; his head slouched forward. His arms were at his sides. He was still holding the Ruger.

For a second, I wanted to run. I spun around. I took deep breaths and composed myself.

As I moved even closer and saw a small, leather-bound notebook on the man's lap. I picked it up and glanced through it. It was a daily journal.

This was the last entry, splattered with blood.

RED

When I was a kid, maybe 12, I used to ride my bike down to Carmen's Creek to go crabbing. I always felt useful when I could bring a couple of crabs home. Sometimes a guy would stop by and buy a couple of them. Between that and the bottles I could find on the side of the road, I had enough money to get comic books and gum.

There was a guy there a lot, crabbing, too. He was dressed in dirty, worn clothes and smelled bad. He had long hair and a scraggily beard. I thought he was tall then, but when I grew up, I realized he was just an average-sized person. We were there a lot. At the beginning, we never said much to each other. He just sat in his frayed folding chair and I just sat on the end of the landing. He had a weird tic. Every once in a while, he would take his right hand and rub it down from his left shoulder to his left hand. He would then take his left hand and rub his right arm. Then he would take off his hat and rub the top of his head.

One day when I was checking one of my lines, he stood up and walked over and held out his beefy, freckled hand.

He said, "I reckon that people who have the same interest and are together a lot shouldn't be strangers."

As I took his hand, he said, "I'm Red."

I shook his hand and said, "Nice to meet you, Mr. Red."

"No Mister. Just Red."

I tried to pull my hand away but he tightened his grip.

"I'm Red," he repeated, "who the hell are you?"

"Oh, I'm Frank," I said.

"Frank," he said, "that what everybody call you?"

"Yup," I said.

"Well, I guess I don't have to call you what everybody else call you. Cause I ain't everybody else. I'm gonna call you… Crabber."

I felt humiliated and special at the same time. No one else ever called me Crabber. Only him.

"Well, at least we ain't strangers no more," he said, and went back to crabbing.

Seems like most summers, I would see him a lot. One day, we were both doing well. Both of us had about a dozen crabs apiece.

"Crabber," he said, "let's go to my place and cook these suckers up."

I had never known where he lived. I was scared a bit, but we had known each other for about a year. And I was hungry. I followed him from the landing through the marsh on a narrow winding path until we came to a ramshackle shack. Stuck out in the middle of the marsh surrounded by rusting junk. He always had his wood stove going so he just put on more wood and put a pot full of water on the stove. We threw the crabs in and they boiled up fine. He dumped them out on his old, beat-up table and we cracked them with a regular carpenter's hammer. He placed his special mix in the middle of the table and we dipped the crab meat and ate. Best damn crabs I ever tasted.

I guess he was a Vietnam vet. He talked about it some. He said he saw too many of his friends come home in those metal boxes. He, he wanted to be cremated. Not locked up in some box in some place next to other people in boxes. He didn't want an address.

One time when I was there, he tried cooking up some eggs. First one he cracked into the pan, turned out to be a dead chick. It stuck to the pan. He cursed and hung the pan back up on the wall and threw the rest of the eggs out into the marsh. That pan with the chick hung on his wall for several years.

I often wondered if Red was lonely. I asked him about it. He said never. He told me that a lot goes on in the marsh. One time, a space ship landed next to his house. He said the aliens looked just like us except they were all beautiful women in skintight clothes. He described them in much detail. He said they didn't speak English, but somehow he could understand them and they could understand him. He was kind of attracted to one of them and took her to bed.

"I was shocked," he said, "she didn't have no place to put it."

"Put what?" I said.

"It," he said. "The thing. You know what 'it' is, right, Crabber?"

"Yeah," I said. I had no idea. I figured "it" out years later.

Once I told him that if he got a job, then maybe he could move into a real house. That got him started. Said he didn't want no damn job and no damn house. Didn't want anyone telling him what to do. Or havin' to get up and be someplace at a certain time. No sir, he was fine with gettin' up when he felt like gettin' up, and sleepin' when he felt like sleepin'.

He once asked me if there were any wires coming into my house.

I said, "Sure. Like everybody."

"Not me," he said. "I don't like wires."

He asked what they did.

I said, "You know, electricity and phones and stuff."

He said, "You sure they ain't puppet wires?"

I finally asked him about his tic.

"Red, how come you rub your arms and your head?"

"Checkin' for wires," he said.

"What wires?" I said.

"Puppet wires. One day, you wake up and someone else is controlling what you do. Don't have much time to cut those wires before they get attached for good."

I got older and went off to college. I didn't see Red that often but every year I tried to get down to the landing. Between my junior and senior year at college, I came home. I was busy I guess, but finally, early one morning, I went down to the crabbing spot. There wasn't anybody at the landing. I just sat there a while. Then I got up and walked along the path to Red's house. It was slightly more overgrown than usual. When I got near, I noticed that there was no smoke coming out of the stack at the top of the shack. I stood outside and as I always did, I shouted, "Red" a couple of times. There was no answer. I pushed the flimsy plywood door and went in. The place was buzzing with flies and smelled awful. Red was on his bed. I guess he had been dead for a couple of weeks.

I searched the place. I knew I wouldn't find anything—at least not the things I was looking for—a driver's license, a bill, a letter, a certificate… All I found, in the drawer next to the stove, was $63 and his dog tags. I left them. I pulled some wood from his pile and stacked it up in the middle of the room. The matches, as always, were in the small drawer. I lit the fire and stepped out of the shack. I stood there for a minute or two to make sure the fire caught.

"See ya, Red," I said.

I turned and walked back down the path. I heard the crackle of the fire and smelled it for a long time. I took off my cap and rubbed the top of my head. I didn't look back.

HER

⋎⋏⋎⋏⋎⋏⋎

1 River

Along the river's empty bank

The warm water, exhausted, almost gives up, and laps listlessly at the flat mud

The air is equally lethargic

I am pinned, fixed, stuck

Not like a beautiful moth in the museum where the young girl says, "oh look, it has owl's eyes"

But like a dusty roach on a piece of recovered Styrofoam tossed in a corner of a boy's dark room

You approach like a light blue kite in a steady breeze, like a dhow on a single tack

Your boubou crisp and shining

You arrive, condensation on your smooth skin, and explode a smile

You pull the pin

I breathe

2 Tea

Everything has retreated from the burns of the sun
Under the mango tree you sit on a low stool making tea on a
small charcoal burner
Silent
Patient
Pouring long lines from the pot into 2 small glasses
Finally, you offer, on a dented tray, a glass
A slight bow of your tressed and partly covered head
My fingers touch the glass and run it across the tray generat-
ing a current to your fingers
You raise your eyes in a question

3 God

For her, God has no children and no face
Yet is always present
In the movement and stillness of the earth
Her devotion is so strong
She senses my unease
Touching my hand
She smiles and says God is God, you are a man

4 Night

Out here the stars are close, dripping, swirling
Out here it is soundless
Out here on the river, small fish jump into the boat
Out here the world is deep and waiting
But the smiling woman is gone

MEMORY

This story is about memory. That strange, unreliable phenomenon. Sometimes we forget, often, in fact. And sometimes we remember inaccurately. Almost never do we remember accurately. Maybe never. All we remember are stories that we tell ourselves. Happy people make up positive stories and remember those. We are constantly tricked by our memories; they have no anchors in reality. Sometimes we even forget the good stories that we have created. We ache to recall them. There is a word for homesickness for a place that we have never been. This story has already forgotten what it is about.

MAD RIVER

"**C**ome on," I say, "it'll be fun."

"Fun," he says, as if he has never heard this word before. "It's too cold. Who will take care of the dog?"

"It's 90. We'll only be gone a couple of hours."

"We shouldn't leave the dog, damn it!"

"It's okay. Don't get grumpy." Never tell a grumpy person not to get grumpy.

"I'm not grumpy. Who will take care of the damn dog?"

"Luther will be fine for a couple of hours. You need to get out. You haven't been outside since the stroke, really."

I gently coax him. But I am worried—he is old, what if something happened? I wheel him out to the car. He transitions to the walker and then to the front seat.

As we pull out of the driveway, I see that Luther has jumped on the couch, levered open the curtains, and is watching us leave through the living room window. He adds to the nose smudges already covering the glass.

We are mostly silent on the drive. When we are halfway to the drop-off point, my father asks if I have checked the stove. I say yes and that I have left three burners on medium-high. He tells me not to be a smart-aleck. He dozes for a while.

We get to the drop-off point—a grassy meadow that leads down to the river. I get the walker and get him out of the car. The guide stands next to a huge pile of pink inner tubes. We sign the waivers. There are six other people on this trip; we exchange hellos and how-are-yous. My dad attracts some attention. The other tubers are still vivid, with dark hair and beards, tanned arms and legs. We are pale and white, slowly fading. They ask about him almost as if he were not there. I tell them he is 93 and is as strong as a mule. As always, he says that being 93 is better than the alternative. They are impressed and wish us luck. They go back to discussing how much beer they brought.

Using the walker, we go slowly down to the water's edge—it is calm and shallow. There is a small sandy beach that makes getting into the water easier.

With the walker, my dad wades into the river a bit. After a slight pause, he says: "I'm getting cold feet."

Everyone laughs.

I say, "You had cold feet at the house."

Now, more serious, he says, "I don't think this is a good idea. We should go home. We shouldn't leave the dog. Someone has to take care of Luther."

"Too late," I say. "It'll be fun."

"It's too dangerous. There might be rapids. And that damn dog."

"There are no rapids. It's like being in a pool but with better scenery. Luther is glad we're gone."

We get a bright pink tube behind him. He says what if he falls through? We tell him that the tubes have netting. He says pink is not his favorite color. In fact, he says he hates pink. All the tubes are pink. I take one arm and the guide takes the other, and we slowly lower him into the tube. He asks if they have another color. We do some adjustments and he seems okay. The guide tethers my tube to my father's with a 12-foot rope. My father doesn't understand why all the tubes are pink.

We have a smaller tube with a cooler for our stuff. The other tubers have coolers of beer. Our cooler has suntan lotion, water, a thermos, adult diapers, a beach towel, his meds, my phone (he doesn't use cell phones), his snack bars, the car keys, paper towels, and the New York Times crossword. He insisted on the crossword in case we get marooned. In spite of the fact that the doctor doesn't want him drinking, I have brought a thermos of his favorite chardonnay.

We start floating. It is brilliantly sunny and hot. Using my arms, I paddle us out to the middle of the broad river. I don't know how this is possible, but we seem to be tubing more slowly than everyone else. The others are soon about 30 yards in front of us. From time to time, I can hear their laughter, but I am sure my dad cannot hear a thing. He asks for the thermos. We take turns drinking.

He asks if I have put on sunscreen. I say yes. He tells me that I really should put on sunscreen. I say I already have. I ask him if he needs sunscreen. He says no.

We pass slowly under the Mad River Bridge. It is an older bridge, rusted, with cracked concrete. I suddenly fear that a piece of concrete or decayed steel will fall on us. I hand paddle us a bit faster.

We are mostly silent. When we talk, we talk about the history of the river and the towns along it. He knows the area well. He has been in the area since college and has canoed the Mad River several times, including once almost 65 years ago. But, I say, I bet he never saw it from a tube. No, he says they didn't tube back then.

The area has had its up and downs. Mostly downs recently. Other stretches of the river used to have mills but these have closed down years ago. Farming on these old rocky soils was always difficult and many farmers have moved on. He admires the lushness of the vegetation. It was not this lush when he was younger, he says. All that damn CO2 that we are pumping into the atmosphere, he says. Forests have come back because people have left or can't fight it any more. He says this exuberant vegetation signals something, relates something, tells some story. Forests are nice, he says, but under their exuberance what do they mean?

We come around a slow bend in the river and there are a few houses with docks. On one, a yellow lab comes out to bark at us.

"Who let Luther out?" he says.

I say, "It's not Luther."

"Luther shouldn't be out," he says.

I say, "It's not Luther."

"Someone has to take care of that damn dog," he says. He says he hopes Luther is okay. I say he is fine.

He is quiet for a long time. His head is back, his eyes are closed and his mouth slightly open.

"Dad?" I say.

"Dad?" I say, louder this time.

I search for the tether. At first, it slips in my hands, but finally I have a grip on it. I yank hard and do not know if I am getting closer to him or is he getting closer to me. Our tubes bump and I anxiously maneuver around so I am next to his head.

He is snoring softly.

I let go of his tube. We float apart, circling each other in ancient 12-foot orbits, slowly drifting down Mad River; nothing between us and the sky.

CLEARING

The village is quiet—not yet fully awake. A few chickens strut about. A dog yawns and scratches his ear. A mist hangs in the air. A woman carrying a blue plastic teapot emerges from a hut and walks around to the back of her compound. At Roger's there is a group of 8 waiting, including two teenagers. Roger's loud voice and energy help to awaken the group. He leads them out into the forest along a broad path.

Frank, the American, is carrying a brand new axe. It is a beauty, the best from a hardware store in Stony Haven, New York. Gabon is a forested country and he knew an axe might be handy. It has a long and gently curving ash handle fitting snugly into a broad metal blade. The blade still has a sticker on it: "Lights Out" by Best Cut. A four-pound head and 35-inch handle. But Frank is, somehow, the only one carrying an axe in spite of the fact that the group is going out to clear land for a field for Roger.

Maybe Frank has misunderstood the purpose of the mission. He asks why no one else has an axe. "It's okay," they say. "Where are their axes?" "We have axes," they say. "But aren't we going to clear a piece of forest?" "Yes, just wait," they say. "Be patient." But Frank feels as if he's been tricked. The group will get to some place in the forest and they will watch Frank try and fell an enormous tropical tree. Maybe it is a practical joke or worse, they are mocking him, he thinks. Putting the naive American with the huge, never-used axe, on the spot.

The forest is misty and damp in the early morning. The understory is not heavy. After about 45 minutes, they pause in a small open space and sit. One of the younger men makes a quick fire and heats *baton de manioc* and peanut sauce for breakfast. As they eat, the mist partially clears and Frank looks around. In the understory, about 10 yards from where they are sitting, at about chest height, he sees a small hanging man, still and silent. He is about to say something to the others and then he spots another hanged man not far away from the first. Then another. There are six or seven of these small men hanging from vines in the mist of the trees—heads bent, gravity pulling the lifeless bodies straight down. It's a mass hanging. A mass murder of small men. Frank looks more closely. He goes over to one of the hanged men. The lifeless body is wood, the bent head is metal. It's an axe. A hanging of small Gabonese axes, tied up in the trees the day before.

Now they all have axes. Frank is reassured by this even though his axe is new and twice the size of the axes held by the others. The other axes are well-worn, with short, straight handles and narrow blades. The hand-crafted handles maybe 20 inches have a dark bronze patina, polished with sweat from rough hands,. The heads are locally made by a black-smith, perhaps from car shocks. They are about half the width of Frank's, and maybe 2 pounds. Unlike his axe, the blades of their axes are inserted in the wood.

When they get out to the area where they will be working, Roger takes Frank over to a good-sized tree. Roger looks around, assessing the forest. "This is good," he says, "cut this one." He takes a couple of hacks at the tree to show Frank at what height and what direction he should be cutting. The height is more about the ease of the cutting and Roger tells Frank that he can cut a bit higher since Frank is much taller. But Roger insists that Frank start at a particular side, although Frank can't imagine it matters very much.

The group is spread out in the forest. There is almost no sound but the steady *thunks* of axe on wood. An occasional grunt. A short sentence. A laugh. It is mainly work. Frank does not know the name of the type of tree he has been given, but within 10 minutes, he thinks of it as ironwood. The outer layers of the tree are white and soft and the cutting easy. But with a jolt he hits reddish heart wood that's like hitting a steel beam.

Frank is slower than the others. He becomes less and less aware of what is happening around him. It is not focus, but a closing off. But he takes heart that some of the group are moving on to other trees, having only cut about half way through the first ones. There is a lot of chopping but no felling at all. Frank thinks: I will definitely finish the job I have started; my tree will fall.

The day warms up, even though they are in the deep forest shade. Frank's breaks become more and more frequent. He is sweating intensely. He struggles. His hands seem glued to the axe. After a time, he pries his hands off the axe and looks at them. He counts the blood blisters—there are 9. Almost one for each finger. He attempts to identify the slacker. He tries to continue. The blisters break and his hands become partly covered in blood, the axe handle is slippery. Roger finally comes over. He takes a few cuts on the other side of the tree. He works much more quickly than Frank does. Finally, he says "good" and tells Frank to stop. Frank insists on continuing. He says he is fine and can finish. Roger says no, Frank needs to stop. He tells Frank to go over to a spot where the younger men are sitting. Frank's hands hurt and he is tired. He feels beaten, without the energy to argue. He does as Roger says and walks away from the still-standing tree, feeling inadequate. He thinks that Roger will continue to chop it down but Roger moves on.

He sits in silence with the younger men and they watch the others at work. The others continue cutting but not a single tree has fallen. Frank takes some heart in this—it's harder than it looks. No one else has entirely cut down a tree either. Although he knows that they have all worked on many trees.

There is more talk now. And slowly, one by one, most of the others come over to stand or sit with Frank's group. There are now only three cutters still working; Roger, Boniface, and Arsene; they are all on the same tree. It's a huge okoume with enormous buttresses. The three have built a scaffolding in order to get above the buttresses and attack the trunk core. They are working quickly. There is some talk and Boniface jumps down and comes over to the group.

Frank's exhaustion leads to restlessness; he feels the need to walk around. He wanders away from the spot where everyone is standing but quickly there are shouts. "Where are you going? Come back. It's dangerous," they says. Wearily, Frank returns, feeling not only tired but like a child. His tiredness has reduced his world to the few impotent and uneasy inches in front of him.

Roger jumps down from the scaffolding and comes over to stand with them. Arsene, the lone cutter now, is a small, lean man clearly respected for his forest skills. Alone, he keeps up a good rhythm but after about 15 minutes, there are some shouts from the group. He stops. Everyone is quiet, listening intently for something. He starts again. After a couple of strokes, he stops and readies himself to jump off the scaffolding. He hesitates. They are waiting for the sounds. He goes back to cutting. Then there is a slight cracking sound, and then some shouts. This Frank understands—"Go! Go! Go!" they are shouting. Arsene throws his axe, jumps down and runs to the group.

The huge okoume cracks again and starts to waver. It leans into the crowns of the two neighboring trees. They are all connected by vines in the canopy. The two that the okoume lean into have been cut halfway through. They crack and lean into their neighbors.

Suddenly, there is an explosion—rumbling, crashing, splitting, flashes of light—the whole forest seems to be crashing down at once. The ground itself trembles. Darkness veers toward light, a kaleidoscope of yellow, green, and red flashes. The noise is so loud, Frank puts his hands over his ears. The crashing sounds are accompanied by dust and branches and tree trunks falling, crashing, bouncing back up and crashing again. The space that Frank had wandered to is a mangled mass of wood and leaves and branches.

But it is the light that is so surprising. Suddenly, a huge gap has opened to the sky and light pours in. Like a revelation. Like a physical epiphany. Energy, pent up from the depths of the forest, is released. Eyes have to readjust. They stand now, suddenly, at the corner of a huge clearing.

Shadows and weariness are converted into light and energy. The heavy curtain is pulled back, a door opened.

A small group of insignificant men in a remote patch of forest on a spinning planet in a remote galaxy throw up their hands and shout as light streams in for the first time since time started.

A domain of forest has been cleared in an instant. After the broken forest stops reverberating, stops echoing, the group of older men, like ants on a brush pile, climb over the heap, cutting branches here and there, helping the pile to settle. Only one of them has actually felled a tree and yet dozens of trees have come down and a piece of forest has been cleared.

After an hour, they are ready to go back to the village. This time everyone has their axe. There is not a lot of talking. Everyone is tired. Frank's hands seem to be permanently curled. And during the walk back, the inevitable dark enclosure, with each tired step, re-descends on him. He returns to his own world of doubts and fears, unable to keep the burst of light within him.

ANOTHER DAY

The Happy Valley Home is outside of Allentown, in a rusted-out valley. A past-its-prime valley—like the people at the Happy Valley Home for Seniors. They are all, including Frank, slowly waiting. They are all thinking: pinochle, meds, field trips to the theatre, strawberry Jell-o. They think: *Is this it? Is this it?*

-o-o-o-o-o-

As soon as they get into Mayumba, Pete and Frank look for a bar on the beach. Their butts are sore; they are sweaty, tired, and thirsty. Ten hours on the rutted, forest roads for the second day. They find a plywood bar in the flat, sandy beach town and stand at the counter and order a pair of cold *33s*. The guy behind the bar turns around and pulls the beers from a pail of water. They stand there sipping "cool" ones.

As they are drinking and talking, they hear behind them, in American English, someone say "back off, motherfucker." They look at each other. They did not realize how good 'motherfucker' could sound. How it could reach across the cultural divide. Thousands of miles from home, in a remote corner of the world, in a country that officially speaks French or a thousand local languages —they hear an American accent—as if it was Plattsburgh. They turn around to look at the folks sitting at the tables. Everyone looks Gabonese.

Pete says loudly in English "I'll buy a beer for the pathetic jerkoff that just said 'motherfucker'."

A short but well-built guy with a big beard and moustache gets up and heads toward them, staggering a little.

"You guys fucking Americans?" he says.

His name is Frederic, but says to call him Freddy. He has a multi-syllable Gabonese last name. Somehow, he was in the U.S. merchant marine and spent a lot of time in ports up and down the east coast of the U.S. One of the main things he seems to have learned is how to swear. When Freddy is speaking English, it is very rare for a sentence not to contain the words 'fuck,' 'fuckwad' or 'motherfucker'. Later that night, Pete and Frank discuss whether Freddy swears in Lumbu or not.

Pete buys him a beer. They ask Freddy where they can stay in town. He says there is a *campement* about five miles inland. They say they are looking more for homes, people with extra rooms. They are into staying with families if possible—because it's more interesting and one learns more about the place. This requires some explanation.

Freddy thinks. He smiles. "I can fucking do this," he says at last. He leaves.

Frank says, "Do you think he's coming back?"

Pete says, "There's beer to be had."

Frank gets antsy as they drink. He convinces Pete that they should take a walk out on the beach. They down their beers, get fresh ones, and walk out.

The bartender protests. "Deposits," he shouts.

Pete turns and shouts, "We'll be back."

They head out toward the surf and collapse on the sand near the edge of the water. Facing the ocean. Watching the sunset.

"There's a whole lot of world out there," Frank says.

"What the fuck are you doing *here*?"

"You know, being here—this is a great place to be right now."

After a pause, he says: "I take it back. I would rather be here with Miss July."

A group is approaching them in the darkness. Someone is shouting their names and saying, 'where the fuck are you?' They get up to meet them. It's Freddy with two women.

Under his breath, Pete says, "Holy shit, it's Miss July. Of the Portly Homemakers Journal."

"Damn. And it's Miss August, from the STD Monthly," whispers Frank.

Freddy introduces them. One is Margaret, and Pete seems to take a shine to her.

"This is Uhlease." Freddy says, indicating the other woman.

"Nice to meet you, Uhlease," Frank says.

They walk back to town. Freddy has arranged everything. Pay what you want. Do what you want. The women are single, temporarily, at least.

Frank follows Uhlease back to her house. It is a simple wooden building. There is no electricity. The floors are earthen. There seem to be four small rooms. There is an outhouse and a cooking area outside. Uhlease shows him where he will sleep. It is a low wooden bed with a foam mattress and clean sheets. It is hidden beneath a mosquito net. She hopes it is okay. He is too tired and too buzzed to care. She leaves a storm lamp and a flashlight and says good night. He crashes.

In the morning, Frank emerges into the sandy yard. On one side is a small table and chair under a mango tree. On the other, under another tree, is Uhlease sitting on a short stool cooking on a low fire.

He greets her and she tells him to sit at the table. She brings him a bowl of *café au lait* and a half a baguette. They talk a bit across the yard. She asks what he wants for dinner. He says he is fine with what she wants. He gives her $20 to go to the market.

He explores the town and meets up with Pete.

In the late afternoon, he heads back to Ullease's house. There is a lot of noise coming from her yard. As he turns the corner, five young kids who are gathered around Uhlease suddenly become very quiet, their eyes widen and they take a step back. He greets them, but they stand stiffly, terrified.

Uhlease laughs and says to them, "This is the white man I told you about. He will not hurt you. His name is Frank. Say hello."

Frank holds out his hand to see if any are brave enough. A little girl is first to take his hand, and slowly the rest shake his hand, sometimes with the left hand. He goes inside and gets the Frisbee from his backpack.

On the beach, he tries to teach them to catch and throw the Frisbee, but there is too much excitement and energy. Other kids show up. Finally, he just throws the Frisbee as far as he can. The kids run after it, unable to judge where it will go, swerving at the last minute like a flock of birds. They tussle for it and, running, bring it back. He throws again, long arcs, with a trailing flock of small, chirping birds. Sometimes, using the onshore breeze he throws the Frisbee out toward the ocean like a boomerang. The kids go screaming after it and as it loops back they end up running to the surf and back as it returns to him. They shout. It's magic.

When they are tired, he leads them back into town. The little girl holds his hand. The other kids peel off to go their separate ways, leaving only him and the little girl to head back to Uhlease's.

She is still cooking and the little girl runs to her and starts to help and to explain the magic of Frisbees at the same time. The little girl turns out to be Elizabeth, Uhlease's daughter. Dinner is seafood: shrimp, fish, squid, and clams, in a sauce on rice—it is delicious. After dinner he asks Elizabeth what grade she is in and what her average is. She says 3rd grade and her average is 12.

"12?' he says "12? You can do better than that. What's your worst subject?"

"Math."

"Alright, let's do some times tables."

He and the little girl read by the weak and flickering light of a storm lamp in the yard. She looks at a flimsy notebook, doing her times tables; while he reads *Cannery Row*. She is curious about what he is reading and they talk about it. When the mosquitos start to get bad, they go into house and get under the mosquito net to continue reading. Elizabeth is quickly snoring lightly. He continues to read, wondering what he should do about the little girl. And Uhlease.

Finally, he picks up Elizabeth and takes her into the next room where Uhlease is getting ready for bed. He says: "I am here for a prisoner exchange—Elizabeth for Uhlease."

Silently Uhlease takes Elizabeth from him and lays her down on the bed. She smiles but says nothing. He returns to the other room and gets into bed, disappointed. He reads for another hour or so before he turns off the storm lamp. Late that night, Uhlease comes into his bed and lies down beside him.

"So how is Miss July?" Pete asks.

"She's good. She's sweet. It's cool. Very comfortable there. No hassles. No tension."

"Congratulations, you have discovered the Switzerland of women. Just remember what they say—800 years of peace and neutrality in Switzerland and what do you have to show for it? Cuckoo clocks and cheese with holes."

Frank asks, "How is Miss August?"

"Good. A little schizo. Full of energy. Curious. But doesn't know who the New York Knicks are."

"Ah. Fatal flaw."

The next day, he heads downtown looking for a store that sells hardware. He buys a Petromax lantern, much more powerful than the storm lamps but still uses kerosene. He buys a package of 10 notebooks and a box of five pens. He looks for crayons and a coloring book and can't find them.

In the evening, he shows Uhlease how to use the Petromax. He gives the notebooks and pens to Elizabeth, making her promise to get at least a 15. With the new lantern, reading is much easier.

That night in bed, Frank and Uhlease face each other, heads propped up on elbows.

"So how do you spell Uhlease?" he asks.

She looked at him as if he were a preschooler. "You're strange."

"No, I mean it. It's such a unique name."

"Do have your pen and paper?"

"Ha, ha"

"Ok. Listen carefully," she says: "A —L —I —C —E."

"Wait. What? ... Your name is Alice?"

"It's pronounced Uhlease."

The next day, Pete and Frank organize a sheep roast on the beach. It is partly to give back to Alice and Margaret and Freddy and Elizabeth, although these people seem to do a lot of the work. They start the pit early and have arranged with the butcher to skin and gut the sheep. They buy lots of charcoal and give money to Margaret and Alice to buy and cook vegetables and rice. They get a case of beer from the bar.

People come by and kids crowd around but there is a lot of food. Freddy takes charge of security and there are shouts of "back off, fuckwad" every now and then.

At the end, they all trudge back to town hauling the remnants of their meal and the empties.

Frank and Alice sleep together. He tells her they are leaving the next day. Her silence absorbs the air from the room.

In the morning, he packs and loads the pickup. His four days off are over. He stands with Alice in the middle of the sandy square. Pete is already in the pickup and ready to go.

Idly Frank says to Alice, "If I stay another day, I will never leave."

She reaches out her left hand and takes his right hand. She gently strokes the back of his hand with her thumb. She looks at him with her soft brown eyes, droplets of sweat on her forehead.

Quietly, she says, "Stay another day."

Pete shouts from the truck, "Holy shit, let's go."

He kisses her on the left check, then the right. "Bye, Uhlease."

He turns and walks to the truck.

In the passenger seat he shivers once. "Thanks, man," he says.

Pete looks at him and pauses. "No sweat," he says.

They begin the hot, bumpy trek back to Okondja.

-o-o-o-o-o-

Late at night at the Happy Valley Home, once the med woman has made her rounds and given Frank his drugs, once the pinochle players have gone to bed, once the coughers have stopped, once the insomniacs have finally settled down, she visits.

She reaches out her left hand and takes his right hand. She gently strokes the back of his hand with her thumb. She looks at him with her soft brown eyes, droplets of sweat on her forehead.

She says, "Stay another day."

MUSHROOM RISOTTO

Ingredients:

2 cups chicken broth, low sodium (for his high blood pressure)
1 tablespoon olive oil
1/4 onion, diced (he preferred purple onions)
1 garlic clove, minced
1/4 pound fresh Portobello and cremini mushrooms, sliced
1 tablespoon fresh thyme, chopped
1 tablespoon butter
1/4 -ounce dried porcini mushrooms, cleaned (optional)
1/2 cup Arborio rice
1 bottle dry white wine (use ½ cup for cooking)
1/2 cup fresh Parmesan cheese (or Romano), grated
Fresh Italian parsley, for garnish, (optional)
Salt and pepper

Directions:

Heat the chicken broth in a saucepan and keep warm over low heat.

Dice the onion and garlic. Good knives are essential, like the ones he gave me for our 4th anniversary. They were beautiful. Heat 1 tablespoon of oil in a large skillet over medium heat and add the diced onion and garlic. Sauté, stirring until translucent, about 6 minutes.

Add the fresh mushrooms, herbs, and butter. For our fresh vegetables, we would go to the farmers' market at Nottaway on Saturday mornings. Sauté for 3 to 5 minutes until lightly browned, season with salt and pepper. Reconstitute the dried porcini mushrooms in 1 cup of warm chicken broth and add. The way the dried mushrooms come back to life when reconstituted is like a small miracle. We never used them before, but I like what they add to the recipe, these days. Sauté 2 minutes then remove from heat and set aside.

With the remaining oil, coat a saucepan on medium-high. To prevent the grains from sticking, add the rice and stir until the rice is coated and opaque, about 1 minute. This is a key step. Stir in the wine and cook until it is nearly all evaporated. For the wine, we would open a bottle of Chardonnay, use a ½ cup, slowly drink the rest.

With a ladle, add 1/2 cup of the warm broth and cook, stirring, until the rice has absorbed the liquid. Add the remaining broth, a little at a time. Continue to cook and stir, allowing the rice to absorb the broth fully before adding more. While I stirred, he would sometimes stand behind me, his fingers lightly touching, his breath on my neck. The risotto should be firm and creamy, not soft and pulpy. Transfer the mushrooms to the rice mixture. Stir in Parmesan cheese (or Romano, he preferred Romano), and cook briefly until melted.

Risotto can be a bit drab; I would sometimes add a bit of fresh parsley for some color.

Serves: 1

ONE PENGUIN AT A TIME

On the way back to port, a man with long hair and a beard opens a large cardboard box on the stern of the boat. He reaches in and carefully extracts a large bird. It is an endangered yellow-nosed albatross that has been in rehabilitation for several days. The man is careful that the bird does not flap around and injure itself. Kneeling, he places it on the open stern of the boat. The bird stands there and looks at the man. It does not seem interested in doing anything. The man says, "Go." The bird stays. Finally, the bearded man softly pushes the bird toward the edge of the boat, forcing it to fly. The albatross takes off, flying very low over the water. For several tense minutes, it looks as though it will not get aloft, but finally, its long wings beating slowly, it rises higher in the gray sky, heading back to where we came.

The man says, "It had such a good time in Luderitz, it's going back!"

Luderitz is a small town, of German origin, on the arid coast of Namibia. There is a Marine Research Station that has a small rehab facility for injured seabirds, mainly African penguins. These endangered penguins are mainly restricted to the waters of Namibia and South Africa. In the morning and in the evening, two men feed the birds. One is the same long-haired, bearded one from the boat. One of his colleagues refers to him as "the furry one" to distinguish him from his younger, clean-shaven, and short-haired partner. They take the fish out of the fridge and, one by one, place a vitamin in the fish's mouths. The vitamins are specially formulated for the birds. The men herd the birds into a corner of the pen and, down on their hands and knees, grab each bird that tries to get by. They collar the bird, pry open its mouth and ram a fish, vitamin and all, head first into the bird's gullet. One bird darts by without eating, seemingly proud of itself. The men know which one it is. Fifteen minutes later, when most of the birds have been fed, the unfed bird seems to suddenly realize that her joy at escape comes at the price of hunger. She comes back to where the men are kneeling and they feed her.

"They must be very eager to be fed," I say.

"Yeah. Some. They are all different. Some run up and beg for a fish. Some sulk like teenagers. Many are grumpy. Some you have to catch and ram a fish down their throats," the furry one says.

"How long does it take to rehab a bird?" I ask.

"Depends, of course, on the problem. Sometimes a month. The problem is that the longer they are in rehab, the more rehab they need. If it's oil, maybe it's a month of rehab, but by the end of that, they have often lost muscle tone and need more rehab. It's tricky."

They proceed to another small enclosure where there are two orphaned "downies," very young birds. They do not have to be corralled. The younger of the men, the "non-furry one," sits with his legs out and a small bucket of fish next to him.

The downies crowd around him eager to be fed—but clearly also eager to be touched, stroked, petted. The non-furry man feeds and strokes them and talks to them. I don't understand what he says, but the young birds seem very impressed. After 10 minutes, he is up and out of the enclosure.

In with the downies is an adult penguin that has had the major parts of its feet bitten off by a seal. It can't get around so well. It has no future. But it's alive, and they feed it and take care of it.

I ask the men if I can take their picture. The furry one says, "I don't know if I want to be in the same picture as this ugly guy." But then they throw their arms around each other with the automatic ease of old friends.

The men are rarely in Luderitz. For most of the year, they live on an isolated, broken rock in the ocean, an overnight boat trip from Luderitz. There is not a level spot on the rock. They live in an old building, partly on stilts, built by guano collectors a hundred years ago. The mining of bird droppings for fertilizer and explosives was big business then and some of the islands were totally mined, dramatically changing the habitat. The barren island, without a speck of green, 7 acres in size, is off the coast of one of the driest and most desolate deserts in the world. It's riddled with caves; a large one divides the island almost in two. If large swells come from the south and enter the cave, the whole island shudders, reinforcing the feeling of fragility and insignificance in the face of nature.

They do not see another person for six months.

"I hope you have a guitar," I say.

"It was tough when I started out. It was only me. There was no electricity. Only candles. Now there are some solar panels and we have lights and all. We now have some radio contact with Luderitz," the furry one replies.

To me, the colonies of penguins seem like undifferentiated masses of random motion.

"When you first see a colony, you are impressed with the chaos and disorder. But after a while, you see how orderly it is. The same birds on the same spots adhering to the same schedule," he continues.

"Do they get used to you?" I ask.

"We are always the strangers, the foreigners. It's their island, their home. It's more like a kind of cranky tolerance. When you walk by, they are always angry and still peck at your legs."

"A thankless task."

"It has its moments."

These penguins mate for life. They are very loyal.

"What happens if one dies?"

"The remaining one usually waits for a while. Maybe after a full season, it finds a new mate, maybe in the same situation, and they become a pair."

The men know the history of guano mining and over-fishing in the area. On some of the islands, guano was 7 or 8 meters deep. It provided ideal nesting for the penguins. By 1900, it had been stripped away. Overfishing, particularly by foreign countries, has depleted the food sources for the sea-birds, and it continues unabated in spite of Namibia's efforts to protect a much larger share of its marine resources. Penguin populations have plummeted. Some people say that a recovery is in process, but the two men are skeptical. It will take many years.

And the climate is changing. Ocean currents are shifting and sea levels are rising. There are huge global shifts that are beyond the control of two men on a small island. The changes are too big to resist or control. There is a small rock in the middle of the ocean off a deserted and desolate part of the coast of Namibia. There, two men are perched in a small nest surrounded by grumpy seabirds. Immersed in their quixotic quest, they chip away at the loss of the wild, one penguin at a time.

THE LONG-TERM EFFECTS
OF LIVING IN AFRICA

Tom sat cross-legged with the others on reed mats under the shade sanctuary of a large tree. Through an interpreter, they were talking with the chief about the village. The daily routines, the crops they grew, the livestock they kept.

Tom noticed that occasionally, from under the chief's pale blue *boubou*, the tip of his member would appear on the mat. Tom tried not to look, and the rest of the group seemed oblivious. From time to time, a fly would land on the dark and cracked skin. The tip was shaped like an arrowhead. It was stitched all along one side. What wound could have caused such extensive damage? Or perhaps, like circumcision, it was a ritual wound?

When the meeting was over, the chief walked them back to their vehicle. Tom took the interpreter aside and said,

"I doubt I can stay here. Did you see the chief's thing?"

The interpreter smiled and took Tom by the arm to the chief. He said something to the chief in Malinke. The chief smiled and proceeded to reach beneath his robes, fumbling for several seconds at his waistband. The air was almost too hot to breathe.

With a proud smile, and with two hands, he produced and offered to Tom, a locally made knife in a sheath. The leather sheath was cracked and darkened, its tip like an arrowhead. It was carefully stitched down one side.

The interpreter said, "Maybe you should stay."

AT THE MUSEUM OF PHOTOGRAPHY

The man was far from home. The Museum is a small one, relatively speaking, maybe the size of a large house. The reception area had a counter behind which stood two young people, a man and a woman. The reception area also had a small bookstore and a gift shop.

The entry fee was $5. The man asked for a senior citizen discount. They apologized. There wasn't one.

The young woman explained: On the first floor, there were two small projection rooms. On the second floor, there was a small exhibit space. On the third floor, next to the offices, was a third small projection room. The projection rooms had narrated short videos showing the history of the place through a series of still photos from the archives. Room #1 covered the landmarks of the town—churches and monuments and memorials. Room #2 had a video on the discovery of the town. Room #3 had a history of the town through family photos.

"Have a great visit," she said.

The museum seemed almost empty. In the first two projection rooms, there was only one other person. In the exhibit space, there was no one.

In projection room 1, the two benches were empty. The slightly yellowed photographs of the landmarks of the town depicted times when life was less crowded and not as fast.

In projection room 2, there was one other person sitting on one of the two benches. The video showed the founders of the town and various stages of the town's development.

He took the stairs up to the second floor. He wandered through the one-room exhibit space from left to right. There were photographs from the studios of the well-known photographers of the town. Many were families posed with prized possessions. A couple holding a baby on a motorcycle. A couple dancing the twist. A family at the beach.

He climbed the creaking wooden stairs to the third floor. The offices were to the right. On the left were the dark blue curtains to the third projection room. He went in and sat on the bench. The room was empty.

As he sat alone in the small room, it got dark and a video started being projected on the wall.

First, there was an old photo of a toddler digging a hole in the sand at the beach.

There was a picture of a boy in a scout uniform.

There was a picture of a basketball team.

There was a picture of a young man in cap and gown.

There was a picture of a young couple.

There was a picture of a baby and a toddler.

There was a picture of a group of people at a workshop.

There was a picture of a man on the top of a mountain.

There was a picture of a family dinner.

Then there was a picture of a solitary man sitting on a bench in a darkened room.

This picture then split in half to show two images, they split to show four, they split to show eight, they split to show 16.

The splitting images became an undecipherable, moving screen that eventually became dimmer and dimmer.

The room became dark again. After a few moments the lights came back on.

When the man left the room, he bumped into a sign that had been placed in front of the blue curtains.

He walked down the stairs to the reception. As the man walked out of the Museum, the young man at the reception area looked at him.

"Very sorry that the 3rd room was out of order. We hope you had a good visit anyway," he said.

INCENSE

Fatima is doing a project on olfactory heritage in Senegal. We decide to go to the market to see if we can find incense. I am particularly interested in ones that can help with relaxation—from the very little I know about aromatherapy. Fatima appears to have other priorities. The taxi drops us off, but the outdoor market is empty, eerily deserted. The stalls are closed, the metal shutters rolled down. Instead of the usual chaotic crush and cacophony, there is silence and space. It is unnerving. Fatima says that perhaps it's because the president has ordered markets to be cleaned on the weekends because of the pandemic. A frontend loader sits ominously at the end of an alleyway. And piles of wood, including pallets that have been repurposed more times than is useful, litter the alleys.

Finally, we see a couple of shops that are open on the main road. Merchandise has spilled from the shops onto the front steps and onto the sidewalk. To get by, you have to walk on the street.

Fatima spots one that resembles the aftermath of a small explosion in a birdhouse factory.

"Let's go," she says, indicating the birdhouses.

I am perplexed. We don't need a birdhouse. We've never talked about birdhouses. We've never talked about birds. We rarely mention animals, except for cats, at all.

"Great," I say.

We climb up the couple of steps crowded with stuff to get inside the crowded shop. There is merchandise covering every inch of the place. Shelves to the ceiling teeming with multi-colored bottles and jars. Stuff hanging from the ceiling, goods covering the pillars. Merchandise on the floor that you have to be careful not to trip over. The "empty" space is filled with customers, all women. There is barely enough space to turn around. I settle in to wait our turn, but Fatima is already engaged with a salesperson—a young and energetic man—able to contort his way through the shop, who seems to be helping three sets of people at once.

I suddenly realize that we are in a seduction shop. The bottles are perfumes and incense, the articles of clothing basically sexy underwear and lingerie. Incense is clearly thought to be an aphrodisiac, a kind of Viagra taken through the nose. The birdhouses are, in fact, fancy incense burners.

The salesperson has a nice small demonstration incense burner, which does not look like a birdhouse, where he drops in different incenses to show clients. I ask for one. He contorts his way back through the shop.

He brings one out. It is nice, not as nice as his, but nice. I ask him how much it is.

"Five dollars," he says.

"Three is good," says Fatima.

"Five dollars," he repeats.

"Three is fine," Fatima repeats. "And we want to buy some incense."

The salesperson silently does a calculation of economies of scale. He doesn't say anything but starts to clear what appears to me to be clutter, but for him, clearly there is a system. He opens up large stainless-steel vats.

The vats are filled with incense; mixtures of herbs, resins, oils, seeds, flowers. Some look like baked beans, some look like pesto, some look like marinara sauce. But they all are incredibly fragrant. There is a conversation that I can't follow about names and types and, I think, uses. Fatima takes some pictures and we get small quantities of almost everything.

There are two vats that the guy didn't open. I open them to see. One is two-thirds full of what looks like creamed spinach but is very fragrant. The other is half full of what looks to be pink sand. We ask the guy what they are. The spinach is another type of incense. The pink sand is sand from Mecca. I ask what one does with sand from Mecca. The query is drowned out in other people's demands and questions, and the clear indication that that is a question not worth giving much thought.

The incense shopping appears to be complete, and Fatima moves on to the "clothing." She has a friend who is getting married and she wants to get her something for her wedding night. She holds a small packet with what appears to be a very small fishnet. It is some lingerie, I think. The picture on the outside shows a curvy white model wearing the net. Her nipples are blurred.

"How about this?" Fatima says, showing me the net.

I have no idea.

"It looks great," I say.

"Maybe I should ask one of the older women in the shop?" Fatima says.

This seems to me to be a bad idea, potentially embarrassing. Why would you ask someone you don't know, in public, about their intimate moments?

"Sure," I say. "Why not?"

She turns and re-enters the store to talk with some of the women customers. I guess it's to get advice on what works on the night of a marriage—what to wear. She comes back satisfied. She has vetted the net.

The net, the incense burner, special incense charcoal briquettes, the incense, and some sand from Mecca comes to about $12 after Fatima reminds the guy that $3 is good for the incense burner. This seems like a bargain.

Five minutes later in the taxi, Fatima discovers that the net is pink. She wanted black. She asks me what I think. I say pink is nice, but I don't know her friend. She clearly wants to go back. "Let's go back," I say. We go back and she runs in to exchange it.

At home, I am anxious to try my new burner and some of the incense. I ask Fatima which incense I should try that night. Out of the five, she selects two.

"There is only one problem," she says.

"What's that?" I say.

"You will be alone," she says.

THE STRANGE PERSON

My name is Sirafin Doumbia and this is a story about a strange person who came to visit us, the people of Rocks-end. When we first saw him, we were confused; he was strange looking. He looked like he spent his life underground or in a dark place. His eyes were pale, we thought he might be blind. We thought he was a male person because he had hair on his face. But the other side said that in the country of the strange person, even female people had hair on their face. Can you believe that? We laughed. God has rules and they can't be broken. Female people do not have hair on their face. But, who knows, there are strange things in the world, and it is a big place, maybe big enough for female people with hair on their face.

Here is a story about what the strange person did. We heard about him from the for'service people. The tall for'service person said a stranger asked if we wanted to work in the forest. The tall for'service person was always telling stories and we did not believe him. But the strange person came to us and met us, the female people of Rocks-end, and said did we want to work with him and for'service. He wanted us to consider, but we had already thought and talked and when we said it wasn't worth it, he looked disappointed. But when we said, when do we start, he was happier. When we were supposed to start, the strange person wanted to talk to us and tell us what to do and how to do it. But many of us were busy and did not understand so we just started. The strange person was angry but then he showed us what to do and that was better. We were happy because we got wood and the fors'ervice people did not bother us as much. This helped the female people of Rocks-end. The strange person did that.

The other side said he was a djinn. He was pale like a djinn and did strange things. Not a normal one and not a good one. But we said he comes to us and he helps us, and he walks like a person and sweats like a person, so how could he be a djinn? They said that one day he would eat our children and very fast we told God not to listen. That was not a thing to say.

When the wife of the person who leads us died, peace be with her, the strange person came out and sat with us. He was quiet and stayed a long time. And then the strange person left. It was good, but the other side said that he was being paid to sit with us. I'm not so sure.

I don't know how people eat in the strange person's place. I know they don't eat like the people in our place. Because between the bowl and the mouth, much was lost, like a little child, or the old man who shakes.

The other side said he must be getting paid lots of money to work in our place. And they said he had money for our place but was keeping it for himself. But I like to wait and see.

I will tell you another thing that the strange person did. He brought to us, to stay with us, a female person from his place. That female person was kind and she helped me build an oven and showed me how to bake small treats. At first, I made money selling the small treats to small people going to school. But sometimes the small people do not have coins. How can you refuse a small person with no coins? This is very hard. And the price of flour and sugar went up. My oven is there, but I do not use it. The female person from the strange person's place did many other things. We talked about her a lot. We were without smiles when she left. That strange person brought her to stay with us.

He said his name and the people from for'service told us, but his name did not suit our mouths. We gave him a name from our place. Except that most people called him Sirafin's stranger. Can you imagine?

Here is another story about what the strange person did. One day he brought a female person from our country. She was a Cissé, but she did not have sharp teeth. She said she would give us money for our plans if first we gave her some money and then paid more money back. It did not seem like a good idea. But we talked and she said we could use the money for a project like donkey carts and pumps. She left and we talked under the tree and the other side said that the female person called Cissé would take our money and not come back and that she was the girlfriend of the strange person and they would leave our place. But I was not so sure. We talked and decided that we would get the money and buy donkeys and two-wheeled carts. To be fair, all the female persons in our group would get one. That was 53. When the female person called Cissé came back, we told her, and she got out a small box and told us that we had to give her thousands in order to get the money for 53. We told her she had misunderstood because how could we have that money? We told her we had said 2, maybe she was not used to how we spoke the words in our place.

We got the money and then had to buy the donkeys but we were scared. What if they died? We asked the strange person to buy the donkeys for us, but he said no. The other side said that showed he did not want to help us. The strange person said we should do it ourselves. We told him we would get lost, but he laughed. He said, what about me? He said I know less about donkeys and where to buy them than you. So we did it ourselves. We got a young male person to take care of the donkeys. We rented out the donkey carts. We paid the female person called Cissé without sharp teeth back before she said we had to. She said she was proud of us. But we were proud, too. The other side said that the female person had tricked us, but we had the carts and we made some money. That was a story about what the strange person did.

At night under the tree, the other side said that there must be something really valuable in our place. Why else would he be here? And once the strange person found it, he would steal it. But what could this valuable thing be? And why would he steal it? I prefer to wait and see.

Sometimes he would come out and we could hear him stop the 4-by-4 and start saying, "Is Sirafin Doumbia here? Where is Sirafin Doumbia?" The children would run up to me and say, "Your boyfriend is here!" Imagine an old married female person like me. A little boy ran by me and said, "Your boyfriend is here." But he got too close, and I took a branch to him, and he never said it again. Ha, I say he was a fast learner.

This strange person gave me a grafted mango tree. He helped plant it in my yard. He told us how to take care of it. I was worried that it would die and the strange person would be angry. But it turned out that only the new part died, but the old part grew very quickly. It gives small, stringy mangos, not grafted ones. I am very glad that the strange person did not notice this.

The strange person only came from time to time, maybe once every three market days. But he tried to help us and never asked for anything, except maybe for us to do things for ourselves. He was difficult to understand. But I like to wait and see.

One day, the strange person came and said he was going back to his country. The other side said it was because he could make more money there. But I am not so sure.

He came to our place one time after that. His mouth was flat and we could not see his teeth. He never came back but he was in our place still, he has a tree here. For us, the female people of Rocks-end, it felt like a long dry season had started. But every dry season ends, and the rains come back. And then there is another one. My name is Sirafin Doumbia and there is more to this story, but that's all I want to say right now.

AISSATOU AND
FRANK'S FATHER

When Frank finally started writing short stories, his father became one of his most faithful followers. Among the stories, his father had a few favorites, mostly those based in Africa. Several of those stories featured a character named Aissatou.

Frank's father liked the story about a small village and a local tradesman who lived there. One line from the story was about how Aissatou and the tradesman might start a conversation around a pair of shoes. Frank's father would often repeat that line, "Maybe they would start a conversation."

When Frank visited, his father he would sometimes say, with a small grin, "Oh, how's Aissatou?" or "Have you heard from Aissatou recently?"

Maybe Frank's father thought that Aissatou was some kind of muse. Perhaps he was asking indirectly if Frank had been writing. Frank would always reply, "It's been a while."

Years ago, Frank lived in Obili, in Gabon, for 17 months. At the periphery of the village, just before the forest, in a decrepit hut, lived a very old woman. She was slight, wrinkled and bent. Sometimes she walked around with no clothes. Her dirt yard was always carefully swept but her house looked like it might collapse at any minute. Many people visited her even though they could no longer understand what she said. They brought her food and filled her water jug since she was not able to go to the stream. She yelled at the children who went by her house on their way to get firewood. No one knew why.

The villagers explained that the old woman was no longer human, no longer a person. That she had already started the journey to the other world. That she was half-angel, maybe more than half. They treated her with patience, respect, and sometimes awe. Her ramblings were not delusional; it was that she had started to learn another language that they could not yet understand.

Perhaps his father had started a similar journey. Perhaps he was starting to speak to other half-angels and demi-spirits that surround us.

In fall of that year, Frank's father had a stroke. As soon as he could, Frank made the trip to upstate NY to visit him. It was late when he arrived, and no one was with his father in the hospital room. The stroke had not been too severe and his father could still talk.

He said, "I got a call from Aissatou last night."

"Dad, how can you get a call?"

"I know it was strange—I don't know how she got this number. You must have told her."

"Dad."

"She is worried about you…both physically and mentally."

"How can 'she' be worried?"

"She says that you need to get in better shape. How are your knees? Are you exercising? If you neglect that, it's all downhill from there. And she said you seemed sad and confused. Are you alright? You need to slow down and take care of yourself. Emphasize the good. Be constructive. Contribute."

Frank talked to his sister.

She said, "He's old, what do expect? There are no longer boundaries on his associations."

"But he is imagining things. He is losing grip on reality. Maybe it's the stroke."

His father seemed to be improving and Frank returned home.

Three weeks later, he got a call from his sister that his father had died.

That night, Frank got a call from Aissatou.

IN A DARK ROOM

In the dark, sparse room he watched as she slowly took off her clothes. Always she took off her scandals first and placed them under the stool. Then she took off her headscarf. Her hair was lush and dark and voluminous. She folded the scarf and placed it on the stool, smoothing it. She took off her *boubou* and folded it and placed it on the stool. She was braless. She untied her *pagne* and carefully unrolled it from around her slender waist. She folded it and put it on the stool, on top of the boubou. She was wearing white underwear. She took them off and carefully placed them on top of the *pagne*.

She came over to where he sat and turned around with her arms behind her back. Her unique smell engulfed him. He bound her wrists with leather straps. Her hands were loose fists. He bound her elbows, gently forcing her back to arch.

He placed the bit in her mouth and buckled the straps tightly behind her head under the masses of hair. He led her to the table and bent her over. He entered her. Her head bounced lightly on the tabletop. They grunted.

Afterwards, he undid the bit, then the elbows, and then the wrists. She massaged her arms for a second. She said nothing.

She went and took a shower. She glistened. She came back to the room and deliberately dressed.

He walked her to the door. As she turned to go, he swatted her butt. She stopped and slowly turned, standing directly in front of him. She slapped him sharply across the face. Her eyes were shiny and hard. She turned and walked away, her hips and ass swaying slightly. He watched her until she turned the corner of the street and was lost from sight. She did not look back. All that remained was the sting. He hoped it would never subside.

THE CHIEF'S ELEPHANT

In a village in Africa, there is a very powerful chief. This chief had a pet bull elephant that he loved very much. The elephant would roam around the village and the surrounding bush. It would also destroy people's crops, scare their children, and knock down their fences. In fact, the elephant was a big problem for the villagers.

Secretly, the villagers met to discuss the situation. They all came together one night while the chief was sleeping.

Amadou said, "We must tell the chief that he needs to get rid of the elephant."

Everyone agreed. But no one could agree on who would tell the chief.

Finally, Amadou said that the villagers would have to speak altogether at the same time. Everyone agreed.

Amadou said, "When we meet the chief and when I say, 'Chief!' we all say together, 'Chief, please, you must get rid of the elephant, it is much too dangerous.'"

The villagers practiced:

"Chief!"

"Chief, please, you must get rid of the elephant, it is much too dangerous."

They practiced three times.

The next day, the villagers assembled to meet with the chief.

They pushed Amadou to the front of the crowd.

Amadou said, "Chief!"

But the rest of the villagers remained silent.

Again, Amadou said, "Chief!"

Once again no one said a word.

The chief said, "I heard you. What do you want?"

Amadou said, "Chief, your bull elephant seems to be very lonely. We suggest that you look for a cow elephant to keep him company."

SCARED TO DEATH

On the way out to the dump, I picked up a six-pack of tall boys. I could feel the gentle rush and relaxation just buying them. In the car, I guzzled the first. I popped the second and drank that a bit more slowly. Drunk driving was the least of my worries.

I knew Aunt Jane had a bad heart and all, but how was I to know how bad it was?

The thing in the trunk was following me around. Literally. Like an evil stalker. Like an albatross with fangs. Like a faithful, hungry wolf. Like the end of a ball and chain. Like one of those invisible fence collars. Except my universe was one inch from my skin.

I tossed the second empty on the floor and popped the third.

Even after I dumped the damn thing, I knew it would still follow me around. Even if no one else ever found out, I would know.

I kept seeing her—standing, her eyes wide and then crumbling into a heap on the deck. I didn't mean it. It was partly her fault.

I popped another as I turned onto Turnbull. I was getting closer to the dump and getting rid of that damn thing.

When I got there, I tossed the empties and popped the trunk. I gathered it and hauled it out to the edge of the pit. I threw that damn bear suit out as far as I could.

OUT OF AFRICA,
ALWAYS SOMETHING NEW

I'm in the domestic terminal at Accra airport. Clearly domestic flights do not have the appeal of international flights. The terminal is fairly small and a bit dusty and basic. Since my flight has been delayed, I search for a place to get a snack. In a corner of the terminal is a small room with glass walls where there are a couple of fridges and some sandwiches. The glass door cases have one shelf of water, one shelf of cola, one shelf that is empty, and one shelf with a few unlabeled small plastic bottles with some kind of juice. I stand at the door. A woman in the back of the room gets up from a plastic chair and hitches up her pants. As she approaches me, I hitch up my pants to tease her.

She gets to me and grabs my waistband, one hand on either side and proceeds to hitch up my pants. I am somewhat taken aback but it was quick and natural.

"Ok," she says, "what can I do for you?"

I say "How much is a bottle of water?"

"3 – 50."

"I'll take one." I give her a 20.

"Do you need change?" She says after handing me the bottle.

"Of course," I say.

"After all the work I've done for you," she says, handing me 15.

I walk away thinking the extra 1 50 was money well spent.

THE DISLOCATED JAW

Amadou and Bouba were on Amadou's motorbike going to visit their friend Soumaila. Amadou was driving and Bouba was in back. The road was very dusty and bumpy. As they were in between villages, out in the countryside, they hit a big bump. Unfortunately, at the same time as they hit the bump, Bouba was yawning. In fact, Bouba's yawn was so wide and the bump so big that Bouba dislocated his jaw. In fact, Bouba's jaw just hung there barely still attached to his head. Bouba had to hold his jaw in his hands and press it to the top teeth.

Upon seeing this, Amadou said, "You will need something to tie your jaw to your head – you can't hold it all day." And with that, started running into the bush to look for a vine to tie Bouba's jaw.

This took some time and Bouba grew impatient.

Finally, Bouba shouted, "If you don't hurry up, I'm warning you, I will just let go."

VILLAGE MEETING,
NORTHERN GHANA, APRIL 2018

Some sit on the gnarled roots of the tree, some sit hunched on benches, elbows on knees, some stand at the gathering's edges (but these were onlookers not participants), some lean on bicycles and motorbikes (also in the back), some stand shifting their weight from their right foot to their left and back, some women sit on the small section of ground that has been cemented, legs out straight in front of them, some sit on plastic chairs which had suddenly appeared, clearly meant for the outsiders.

The air is hot and humid; it hangs amongst us like an unwelcome cloak, only stirring occasionally, as panting chickens and an exhausted dog pass by. Time slows and some people sleep or doze. The shadow of the tree slowly shifts and, just as slowly, people move benches and chairs and bikes and motorbikes closer to or to newly shaded ground. There is drumming in the background; perhaps a birth or a naming or a coming of age, but not a marriage or a death.

Some old men sit together with their short white beards, their brimless caps, their plastic scandals; for some, their remaining teeth are highlighted by the gaps that surrounded them. Some of the women hold babies or young children who squirm and whine and hold crackers, but mostly sleep. The position of each in the village can hardly be deciphered by the clothes or position, but as the meeting goes on, centers of power and respect become evident.

People raise their hands and stand and talk, and sometimes there is clapping and sometimes there is laughter. Information is exchanged and provided, some decisions are made and people introduced in their new roles, and sometimes they smile. People give their points of view and share their knowledge and make requests, sometimes real, sometimes not.

The trajectory of the meeting starts its downward descent as women stir, pulled back to the routines of life, anxious about the chores that remain to get done and the children that have to be fed, the water that needs to be fetched, perhaps the advice that has to be given to wayward daughters, and the food that has to be prepared for the evening.

Concluding remarks are made, people jockey for the last word, thanks are given, we stand, small groups form as people disperse, some groups catching up, some analyzing the meeting, some talk with us as we walk to the car. Hands are shaken, some blessings given, perhaps a joke exchange or some teasing done. We leave them to go about their business, their chores, their problems and successes, their laughter and their tears, returning to their routines as we return to ours.

Time has gone by, an infinitesimal and insignificant piece of history has been made, and perhaps a very slight divergence has been created toward a different future.

GOOD LUCK

Dusty dirt road, rural area, northern Ghana. Suddenly we come up behind a large group on the road—children in uniforms. Marching. Chanting. Some have tree branches. Some have signs. It is a protest of some kind. I am nervous because I have been through this before. It can be dangerous. It can be fragile. It can be an emotional storm with no moorings. We inch our way through the crowd, windows up. I look out for people bending over to pick up rocks. I know it is, "Death to America." We inch further and further along and I can see the front of the signs now. I laugh. They say, "Say No to Sex." After a long sigh, Stella, from the back seat, says, "Good luck with that."

THE EASY DIVORCE

She said she wanted a divorce. He said ok. They used a mediator. Their kids were grown and didn't care. They sold the house and split the sale price. They split his pension. They each took a car. They didn't argue much. She didn't even have to go to court. The judge asked him three questions—yes or no. In the hallway, the lawyers talked about the traffic. It had been easy to end things.

And, in the end, he found even turning on the oven was easy, too.

n+1

He thought maybe it would be a good day. The morning terrors had been short because he had to get up to pee, and the stream was fairly clear. He thought that was a good sign, but he wasn't sure since the science was all over the place. He rinsed his mouth with Cool Mint, not looking at himself in the mirror. He found that taping self-improvement lists over the mirror helped a lot—he never read the lists, but they blocked him from seeing himself, and that was always a good thing. Always. Then, the plain bagel didn't burn in the toaster oven—thank god they had a timer—and the low-fat cream cheese went on quite nicely, actually, and he wondered as he did every morning for whom was he even doing the whole-grain and low-fat thing? He decided that he must care about something, but just what that was, he wouldn't be able to tell you. He checked his email, knowing that there would be nothing from his daughters—they had their own lives—and nothing from *her*. Just three emails from Forever Pet Rescue Foundation, one from the AARP, one offering deals on hotels—their algorithm hadn't figured out that he never traveled anymore, and so he closed the computer and then headed off to work looking forward to the subway ride where everyone else looked like he did, like that scene in *Invasion of the Body Snatchers*, only it would turn out that he was the only one who was a zombie, and at work he could hide until Jim asked if he was eating today and he said no. The thing that really shook the day up, though, was when Laura came in and asked him for a recommendation, and at first, he was flattered, and then he saw she was desperate. He said, sure I'd love to, but please draft something that I can use, and she went away, so he wasted the afternoon on the final report. On the way home he wanted the subway ride to never end so that he didn't have to go back to his apartment, but it did like it always did, and he put Hungry-Man Selects Classic Fried Chicken frozen entree in the microwave—thank god they had a timer—and sat and waited for the game to come on so he could watch the mediocre Senators have a mediocre season and lose in the first round of the playoffs. Still, it was something to do, and the game ended at around 9:30 when the Senators lost after leading the whole way. He finally opened his computer and checked his email knowing that there would be nothing from his daughters, nothing from *her*, three emails from the Rescue foundation, an email saying he might have already won a prize, one offering deals on tickets—they hadn't figured out that he never traveled anymore—a special offer from Walgreen's, and he realized he had been wrong. It had not been a good day—not really so good, after all—it was just another day.

ZARANMODIAL

I.

- Let's get another pitcher.

- So yeah, it's so weird. I was feeling pretty drained and not very creative, you know. Like everything was just flat. That there was no juice. No sparks and no building. No new stuff. Just the same old, same old. Going through the motions.

- Happens to us all. Keep drinking.

- Yeah, Pete, you should know. But seriously, I couldn't do anything that sparkled and so I started thinking about it, you know, the times you get into flow and how to make it happen.

- So, do you think you can force flow? Can inspiration be forced? Kind of counter-intuitive.

- Maybe not forced but certainly the conditions for it can be created. You know, just by sitting down and forcing yourself to write. It's shit at first, but if you're lucky, you hit a stride.

- Limited, but yes.

– I see it as the fact that our creative mind is always there, but in most cases, something is controlling it, stifling it.

– Something, like…?

– Something like the part of the brain that is realistic, helps you get through the day. It doesn't like creativity. So it stifles it. Creativity is bad for survival. It needs to be controlled. There is a constant battle. It's driven out by evolution.

– Hmm. Frank, it sounds like your creative center is working pretty well.

– In the brain, there is a part that is the plodding regulator. It makes sure you pay attention to where the danger is, where the predators are, where to get food. To keep your guard up.

– And sex.

– And sex. The plodding regulator is always there, controlling the illusions and dreams and fantasies. These do not help survival. It's Darwinism.

– So, what's to be done?

– I found that you can distract the plodding regulator. You give it some task. And then while it's distracted, the creative part can come out, if only partially.

– Like what?

– Like long-distance driving. When I was driving down to the Keys, the regulator was preoccupied with keeping me on the road. The creative part started working closer to the surface. I wrote my best stuff. Came up with the best ideas. There are other things like that: washing the dishes, mowing the lawn.

- Drinking. Or drugs.

- No. Drinking just slows everything down. You got to get into the zone and create the conditions for the bright lights to come out.

- I like drinking, anyway. It lets certain inhibitions slide. But if your technique works so well, why are you complaining?

- Because I think the plodding regulator catches on, eventually. Eventually, it understands that this is what you are doing and re-asserts itself.

- I don't think my regulator is that strong. I think my creative part is just weak or non-existent. Good thing I have a day job.

- What if you could permanently get rid of the regulator? Would you do it?

II.

- The vision you see—it seems so harmonious, right? It seems so unified. One perfect perspective. But in reality, it is the fusion of dozens of different perspectives. And not just physical perspectives and not just dozens. Maybe hundreds of emotional and spiritual and intellectual perspectives. Thousands.

- But, Doc, how can that be? We are not thousands of bodies, we are one body with one viewpoint.

- No. It's like vision. The image that appears on the retina is upside down. But we see it right-side up. We don't even think about it; it happens. Out of many perspectives, there is one that is fused and seems natural, seems harmonious, seems us.

— Yes, but that is different than saying we are the fusion of different viewpoints.

— Ok. What happens with vision is just to let you know that we do tremendous amounts of unconscious processing and decision-making. And it just seems like reality.

— But the different viewpoints?

— Actually, not just different—conflicting. Conflicting views of the world in your brain and yet, like vision, it just seems unified and harmonious. Parts of your brain fight with each other.

— Fight?

— Disagree. Fight. Argue. Surgeons severed the links between the two hemispheres. One controls verbal, one controls motor. When the person was asked what they wanted to be as a kid, the person responded 'nurse'. When they gave the person pen and paper, she wrote 'actress'. Same physical person. Different and conflicting personalities.

— Schizoid?

— No. Frank. Normal.

— So is there a specific part of the brain that regulates things? Control things?

— Well, yes and no. The brain is very dynamic and fluid but there do seem to be areas of the brain that are more heavily involved in regulation than others. In making sure things don't go off the rails—at least not too much.

– And areas that are more creative?

– Yes, that seems to be the case. There are areas where there are no holds barred. But the regulatory areas tend to keep these areas in check.

– Would it be possible to say, remove the regulatory part?

– I don't know. The brain is just too fluid and dynamic. These are just general areas. The brain can also rewire.

– So what do they do for, like, a brain tumor? They get rid of that right?

– Yeah. But you have a healthy brain. But for tumors, there are a couple of options, most common is targeted radiation.

III.

– I can't believe you talked me into this. If we are caught, we are so screwed. Imagine the headlines. 'Man breaks into cancer clinic to perform radiation treatment on healthy brain.'

– Man and accomplice. And I can't believe you say that every fucking time. It's been what: three times a week for three weeks now?

– Still, it's so fucking illegal, you know.

– And I'm so fucking paying you, you know.

– Just sit in the chair and be still. I have to let the machine warm up.

- Yeah.
- I see you are losing some of your hair.
- These treatments will do it.
- Do you feel ill at all?
- Actually, I feel pretty good for someone undergoing radiation treatment.
- Ok, the machine is ready. Take the position.
- Ok. What is it, five minutes?
- Yeah. I wonder what would happen if we got caught. I don't think you are paying me enough.
- I'm paying you plenty. Just use the damn machine. This is the last treatment.
- Do you feel different? I mean, is your thinking different? I mean, we are destroying a piece of your brain.
- I think I am smarter but maybe that is just psychological.

IV.

- Hey, nice to see you.
- You too.
- Thanks for the recent submissions.
- Yeah.
- Why are you wearing a ski hat? It's like 90.
- Just like that. New style. So, tell me about my recent stories.
- Well, the bad news is that we can't accept them. They are just not right.
- Why not?

– The problem is that crazy—inventing your own language, syntax, grammar, vocabulary—that only you understand—can only be done once. The non-understandable is uniform. You don't get it, you don't get it. There are no shades of not getting it. You don't not get it to the right or to the left, blue or red. You just don't get it. The first time that's done, the point is made. There are things we don't get. But you can't do it over and over. Reality or something approaching it, however has a million nuances.

– But it's innovative. It's out of the box. It goes beyond the normal rituals of writing. It breaks boundaries. You always said that you wanted that.

– I'm sorry. We just can't take these stories. We took 'Zaranmodial'. You only get to be crazy once.

WHO WATCHES
THE WATCHMEN?

We sat in a wooden boat powered by an outboard motor. We followed the shoreline, past villages nested in the steep hills that bordered the lake. We passed small open fishing boats coming in from fishing with lights all night. As we got closer to the Gombe Park headquarters, we saw baboons strolling on the occasional sandy stretches of the shoreline. Mostly, they were solitary, sometimes a small group. They seemed to like the beach.

As we approached the base camp for the research station, the presence of the baboons and red colobus monkeys became more evident. We coasted into the landing site, avoiding the dock for some reason, and beaching the boat directly on the sandy shore. We clambered out. There were baboons everywhere. To go from one building to the next, to walk on the paths, one had to give way to the baboons— some with babies on their backs.

"Don't worry," Deos said. "They're habituated."

"Are they habituated or are we habituated?" I said.

This seemed to inspire Deos to tell this story.

An American researcher was about to leave Gombe and return to the U.S. after many years of research on chimp behavior. He was packed and ready to go, and he decided to pay one last visit to the chimps. He chose to visit Frodo's group. At the time, Frodo was a young aggressive, energetic male who seemed to enjoy bullying everyone.

After hiking for about 45 minutes, the researcher saw two members of Frodo's group about 20 meters off heading through some trees. He started to move in their direction when Frodo suddenly appeared in front of him. Frodo stood erect, his hair puffed out, he hooted. Frodo charged at the researcher and the researcher was not sure if it was the surprise as much as the physical contact that knocked him over backwards. He landed butt first, then shoulders, then head. In an instant, Frodo was squatting over him. He lay as still and quietly as he could. Frodo's face seemed huge as it loomed over him. Frodo looked intently at his face for several moments and then looked around, surveying the scene. Frodo looked down at him again, staring at his face. Frodo looked at his shirt and then looked around. He looked at his pants and belt, and then surveyed the scene again. He looked at his boots. Frodo looked back at the researcher's face, without expression. With his forefinger, Frodo poked the man's torso twice and paused. Then, looking intently at the man's face, Frodo pushed the side of the man's face with his forefinger. Frodo then got up and moved about 5 meters away and squatted on the ground. Frodo could cover the distance in a second, but it was enough for the researcher to slowly get up. He did so and turned and walked slowly back to camp.

The researcher felt as if he had been captured, observed, released.

FIVE BIRDS

She struggled through the sand. Her legs felt heavy and, for every step, it seemed she had to pull her leg out of a sandy hole. She pulled and then placed her foot into the sinking sand. Over and over. She tried to make it closer to where the water was—it seemed harder and flatter there.

Finally, near the water line, it was easier and she walked northward, glancing at the sunset setting behind the dusty horizon. The sun was not going down with a blast of color but slowly fading in gray-orange dust.

A tall, skinny boy approached carrying a large wooden box by a handle. The box was a wooden frame covered in wire screening. There was sharp and active movement inside the box and flashes of bright orange. It was not until the boy came closer that she realized the box was completely full of small finch-like birds—orange-billed *quelea*—all very much alive.

"Wish Birds! Wish Birds! Free a bird and make a wish!" he sang.

"How much?" the woman asked.

"1 bird, 100," he said, "or special Valentine's Day price: 5 birds, 500."

"Quite the deal," she said.

"Isn't it?" he said. "Just for you."

She thought for a second and then opened her small brown purse. She knew what was there, but she studied it anyway. Next to the coins was an old, folded-up 500-franc note. She thought, "This is a good investment." Still, she hesitated.

"Great way to get rid of your sins," the boy said.

"Ok," she said. And gave the boy the old bill. "But only the luckiest birds, not the used ones."

The boy put his hand through a small opening in the mesh, felt around and pulled out a bird. He handed it to her.

She took the small bird in her right hand. Almost unconsciously, she felt her belly with her left hand.

"Don't say it out loud," the boy said.

She said to herself: *I wish the baby is healthy and happy and turns out to be someone good, famous, and powerful.* She released the bird and it bolted toward the east.

The boy gave her the second bird. She thought for a moment. She knew negative wishes never came true. So she said to herself: *I wish my baby and I find someone to love us and treat us well.* She released the bird, and it flew off toward the east.

The boy gave her the third bird. It was smaller than the others. Its beak was less orange than the others. Before letting it go, she thought: *With this bird and this wish, I hope that my mother can accept what I have done and will take me in.* She let the bird go and it flew a few yards off and landed uncomfortably in the sand.

The boy said, "Don't worry. Just resting." And after a moment, it also flew off.

He reached back into the box and pulled out another bird. As he handed it to her, she failed to grasp it fully and it struggled free and flew off before she could formulate a wish. She looked at the boy and thought about asking for another bird, but she remained silent.

The boy handed her the last bird. It was missing some feathers from its left wing. It bit down hard on her forefinger, surprising her. The other birds had not bitten her. She looked at the bird in her hand. She said to herself: *Bird, your wish is to be free, that is the most important thing for you. What will you wish for me in return?* She released the bird and, for a second, it continued to bite her finger until it realized it was free. It lifted off and started its jerky flight off toward the west. She watched it until she lost it in the setting sun.

JUST A LITTLE RUSH BABE

He entered.

Slowly at first.

Carefully with hesitant steps.

But the land gave way. Under an ebb tide as it retreated to gain strength in the accelerating movement of molecules to rearrange themselves from plain worm to brilliant flyer as the huge dark forests lit and burned. And her hyenas lunged against their chains drooling and snapping breaking free to bite with painful vices the exposed heart beating against all reason the fires burned at the head of the water volcanoes noisily destroying in the heat and light crushing smashing rumbling and murmurings beating darkness as the spiral down blasting wanting more skin stripped to nerve ends and the frustration leaping like a deformed frog smashed crashed.

SHE

Crashed and wrecked on the arc burst and red arrows down the movement of the planets floating in a vat of senseless anger. Turned to flash energy, checked the hurtful moon as it satanically beat on the piers of the last port, exploding inside and beyond the narrow closed world of blasted into a thousand centers flying between themselves as they loved and spun in the air, not seared and beaten in a thousand anvils of hope as it crumbled and mumbled. Scratching at the last handhold as descent unstopped in the sounds of voices and scuttling along the bottom of the sea as it reproduced smells from rotted corpses.

Flyer with twisted and scarred wing.

Slowly at last.

He merged.

CONVERSATION WITH PORCUPINE

Hiking up a rocky, slight incline, he grabs a branch to steady himself, but the branch breaks off and he almost falls. His pack is too top-heavy—he has never learned to pack it right. Thirty feet on, he steps on a bare root and almost slips. He turns in frustration and kicks at the root. This time, he slips for good and tumbles backward. His back is protected by his pack, but his right thigh comes down hard on a slightly protruding boulder. He tries to get up but he is so off balance and his backpack is too heavy that he can't. He struggles and attempts to power through, but he is pinned like a butterfly on a board.

He lies there for a moment and shouts, "fuck" as loud as he can. He unbuckles the pack, and leverages himself up. He picks up the pack and puts it back on. He continues on toward the lean-to, hurt and angry. Typical, he thinks—nothing is going right. There is no one at the lean-to. As soon as it begins to get dark, he checks the fire, and climbs into his sleeping bag.

He awakens suddenly in the endless darkness. He can scarcely inhale. It is as if something was sitting on his chest.

At first, he thinks he must be having a heart attack in the isolation of the Green Mountains. Or maybe, he thinks, as he struggles to breathe, it was some kind of stupid panic attack. Typical for him to be panicked in the middle of peaceful mountains with no one around. On the last night of his hike.

He notices that it has started to rain heavily.

Progressively, he comes to the realization that there is, in fact, something, something real, sitting on his chest. He sees nothing in the darkness but hears a slight respiration and feels the rhythm of breathing that was not his own. He is on the verge of panic but lies as still as he can. All he can see are a fleeting few stars among the rain clouds in the sky in front of the lean-to.

The breath of the thing smells like birch bark and club moss, with a remembrance of damp cave. He tries to relax and remain calm, but slowly he becomes terrified. He imagines a bear or a wolf, canines gleaming, surrounded by the rest of the pack. He feels the lull before the inevitable powerful lunge for his throat.

He had not expected his hike to end like this. He had looked forward to twelve days on the Long Trail in the Green Mountains of Vermont, alone in these old, worn mountains. These rolling, introspective mountains suited to contemplation. But there was something also difficult—the slow hours of being by yourself and confronting your own thoughts. In the end, it encouraged an internal life and self-doubts that were maybe not threatening and dangerous; but stupid, immature, and wasteful.

He slowly moves his hand out to where he thought his flashlight must be. The weight on his chest shifts. He freezes. He waits. After several minutes, he continues groping for the flashlight. He does not want to scare whatever it is; for fear that it would react and attack him. He points the flashlight at the back of the lean-to. Finally, he is able to turn the flashlight on and immediately, whatever it is, recoils slightly but remains camped on his chest. With the indirect light, he sees a small dark face with very small black eyes. Behind the head are what appeared to be dozens of horizontal white lines. They are, in fact, quills. It is a porcupine.

The porcupine seems disinclined to move. They lay there together in the obscurity and wait.

This problem does not want to go away, it seems. After what seems like a quarter of an hour of this standoff, he begins to shift his weight. He feels the feet of the porcupine tense. He speaks softly but the porcupine remains on his chest.

He imagines a swipe of the tail and a profile full of quills. This would be quite dangerous. Dawn comes at 6:54 and it is still pouring. His stalemate with the porcupine cannot continue. Finally, he succeeds in rolling over and slips out from under the creature. He scampers on his hands and knees to the other side of the lean-to as fast as he can—he would even jump out if it weren't for the rain. He realizes that he is hyperventilating and forces himself to breathe more slowly. Meanwhile, the animal, seemingly more inconvenienced than scared, lumbers off to the opposite corner of the lean-to. The man gets up and sits on the edge of the lean-to to looking at the rain—him on one side and the porcupine on the other.

His breathing finally returns to normal. They silently watch each other for a while before he realizes that it is his fault—you cannot expect a porcupine to break the ice.

"You are so damned lucky—such a lucky bastard," he says finally.

There is no response.

"See? You don't even feel obliged to answer. You have no obligations whatsoever. No rules of politeness, no customs, and no traditions to tell you what you ought to do. Your world is predetermined and for that, you are one lucky son of a bitch. The rest of us have options."

The porcupine, looking out into the rain, shifts slightly.

"Your entire world is run on instinct. You never ponder a decision. You never vacillate. You never are filled with regret even before a decision is made. You never make mistakes, you never let people down, and you never think that you should have done something else." He thinks of his conversation with his sister before he left on the hike. She knew him better than anyone. She called the hike a "sulkabout".

"I bet you don't even remember your mother or father. Maybe you never even met your father. I cannot escape mine. He is constantly with me, constantly judging me and finding me inadequate."

He can barely see the small trees at the edge of the lean-to clearing.

"If a hedgehog knows one big thing, then what does a porcupine know? You must know even more, an even bigger thing, right? So what is that one huge thing? Total focus or total obliviousness?"

The porcupine appears to be dozing.

"But who is happier? Does the porcupine regret the things he doesn't know? Do foxes regret not doing one thing well? I can tell you about foxes, the little prince's flower says that people have no roots and that bothers them a lot. Always being blown about by the wind. That's the fox."

It stopped raining. The porcupine looks about and finally climbs down from the lean-to and slowly makes his way across the clearing to the woods and disappears.

He packs his backpack. He waits 30 minutes to let the ground dry a bit. The final hike is not so bad—only about 7 miles.

He senses he is getting close to the trail head and where he parked his car. The trail broadens and becomes much smoother. He begins to feel light-footed and relieved. He is energized. The sun is out and he is surrounded by sparkling green. He has finished the hike, he is home. He has survived the porcupine and left it behind.

As he comes onto the small parking area, he sees his car and immediately senses that something is wrong—his front tire is sitting on its rim. As he gets closer, several short dark shapes lumber off into the woods. He sinks to a squat on the gravel, his hands out in front of him. He examines the tire more closely. The sidewall, caked with road salt from the winter, had proven irresistible to the porcupines.

They have chewed large holes in his tire.

SUNSET PIER

"**W**hen does he get back?"

"I told you. Tomorrow."

"Yeah. I keep hoping."

"Look, you're a great guy…"

"Hey, don't 'great guy' me…"

The singer on the small stage speaks. He has a voice like Otis Redding.

"We have a special request from Frank to that special lady." The singer starts to sing "I Thank You."

With a wry smile she says, "Special lady?"

"His words, not mine," he protests. "But I wanted to thank you—you didn't have to, but you did."

"Don't 'thank you' me. It was mutual."

"I can thank anyone I want, without your permission."

The remnants of the sunset hang in the sky. The lights from Tank Island from a short string on the horizon.

She excuses herself and is gone for 10 minutes.

When she gets back, the singer says, "I've just got another special request from the special lady for her wonderful friend." He starts to sing "Ooh Child, Things are Gonna Get Easier."

"Wonderful friend? What kind of bullshit is that?" he says. "And how are things going to easier?"

"His words, not mine," she says.

He wonders what her words were, but does not ask. He does not know what to say.

"How's your mom these days?" he asks.

"She's okay. Such a downer visiting her. Like starting from scratch. The ones we love become strangers."

"Yeah, I know. For everything there is a season. Even love." It's back around to that so quickly.

She has finished her Long Island iced tea. He asks if she would like another drink. She says no. He touches her arm, feeling the downy hair. She pulls away slightly, just out of reach. She hesitates but then says she has to go. Ok, he says. She gives a brief, weak smile and turns and walks away. He follows the outline of her hips, the billow of her shirt, the flow of her hair.

She disappears into the crowd. I am rooted to my chair. I rotate my beer three times. I finish it. I look down into the water off the edge of the pier. Seven or eight pale ghosts of fish ease by under the surface, suddenly vanishing, leaving nothing but the endless black sea.

ANOTHER TAKE

She brings her hands to her mouth and says, "Oh God. Oh God."

Then she says, "No, No. Let's try it again."

She widens her eyes, brings her hands to her mouth and screams.

"Better?" she asks.

"Yeah, let's go with that," he says.

Later that night, she calls her daughter in California.

They talk. The daughter is not doing so well in school.

A discipline problem, they say.

She asks if everything is okay.

The daughter says yeah.

She asks about the grades.

The daughter says nothing.

She asks why it is so difficult to get decent grades.

The daughter says, I don't know, Mom, maybe I'm just not like you.

She says, that's not the point.

She asks about the smoking and the fight.

The daughter says nothing.

She says that smoking is bad for her, not for anyone else.

The daughter says I know.
She says that getting a good education is key to doing what you want in the future.
The daughter says, yeah.
She says getting a good education is the key to being happy.
The daughter says, can I go now. I have something to do.
She says, but we need to talk.
The daughter says, maybe you need to talk. I don't need anyone controlling me.
The daughter says bye and hangs up.
To no one, she says, "Wait. Wait. Let's try that again."

THE STONEYHAVEN ANOMALY

My dad wanted to be a lot of things. He had lots of projects going on all the time. Most were partially or entirely forgotten at various beginning stages. When my dad became older, he threatened to become a writer. He was in his 80s and pretty much immobile, so he had time to think. Becoming a writer made sense since he could not move around and partially build things.

We were on his deck in the summer. It had an unfinished railing that was started 12 summers ago.

"I'm working on a short story," he said.

"Oh. What's it about?"

"Nuclear energy."

"Okay. What you got so far?"

"These government scientists working on nuclear energy and subatomic physics discover an anomaly. The story is called *The Stoneyhaven Anomaly*. They are government scientists working at a national lab with university researchers. Top secret. Very dangerous stuff. Potential catastrophe."

"Has a name like a thriller or mystery, like *The Eiger Sanction*, *The Stoneyhaven Anomaly*! Have you thought of film rights? Now a major motion picture! Starring Denzel Washington!" I tried to sound like a thriller would sound.

"Right," he said sarcastically. "Kind of a scientific thriller. But strong on the science. Educational. Not dumbing it down."

"So what's the anomaly?"

"The kind that puts everything in doubt. Our understanding of the universe. World safety. Humankind. Global annihilation. We are on the cusp."

We watched sparrows on the birdfeeder.

He continued. "There is tension. Fear. A small group of people racing to understand what is going on before the disaster happens. Running through options. Problem-solving. Searching for insights."

"So another understanding of the universe?"

"Yeah."

"So, a new Grand Unifying Theory?"

"Hints of a new GUT."

"So, do you actually have a new GUT—new theory of everything?"

"Well, not yet."

"That seems hard—to lay out a new theory of the universe in a short story called *The Stoneyhaven Anomaly*. And ambitious."

"Maybe."

"Maybe it looks like an anomaly but actually it's something else?"

"Like what?"

A squirrel ran across the railing and jumped off at the unfinished part.

"Maybe a mistake. It could be just a mistake. Like some dust on the monitor, or a mouse in the reactor. Or someone left their sandwich in the cyclotron. Or maybe there was a booger on the radar screen. Or a cleaning lady disconnected the accelerator so she could sweep… It looked like a transformational anomaly—the kind that sets up and leads to a new understanding, but in the end, it could just be a mistake."

He grunted. "No. An anomaly; not a mistake. It's not called *The Stoneyhaven Mistake*."

"Or maybe the anomaly was social. The anomaly might not be scientific or physical. It could be social. Maybe it was group hysteria and imagination. Like a witch hunt. They latch onto a piece of evidence but collectively misinterpret it and panic."

"No, it's a hard anomaly, not a soft one. It's not called *The Stoneyhaven Hysteria*."

"Or it could have been sabotage—no anomaly at all but evidence planted by foreign spies… Turns out it's a spy thriller. Secret agents had planted some fake evidence, switched out some x-rays, or some graphs…"

"Not like that. A true anomaly, not an irregularity."

"So more like a paradox than a contradiction. That is a tall order."

"Yeah, but I'm working on it."

"You know, I think there are maybe three or four grand anomalies."

He grunted skeptically.

"The first great anomaly is why is there something and not nothing. Nothing is perfect in and of itself. Why does nothing need something? Nothing is fine."

He grunted skeptically again.

"The second great anomaly is why there is life and not just stuff. Why do rocks and matter and stuff need life? They are perfectly fine without it. Why did a bunch of dead stuff combine to make life? Who needs that?"

He grunted skeptically again.

"The third great anomaly is why is there consciousness and not just life. Life is perfectly fine without consciousness. Just reproducing mechanically, biologically. In fact, it's probably better off without consciousness. Why would life find it necessary to think about itself?"

He grunted skeptically again.

"The fourth great anomaly, it hasn't happened yet, is why is there a short story called *The Stoneyhaven Anomaly* and no short story at all? The world is perfectly fine without it. In fact, probably better off. Like before, there was nothing and now there is a short story called *The Stoneyhaven Anomaly*. Out of nowhere, out of nothing. Maybe the anomaly is that this short story exists at all."

"Good luck with that."

"Somehow I doubt that there will ever be a short story called *The Stoneyhaven Anomaly*. It would not be an anomaly. It would be a miracle."

"We'll see," he said.

THE LETTER WRITER

From broad concrete steps of the old colonial post office in central Bamako, he saw her approaching and looking around. She wore a pale blue boubou, not new but freshly washed, the fold lines clearly showing. It had white embroidery. She saw him, and she came over toward where he was sitting. She said,

"Greetings. I hope the night was peaceful. Are you a letter writer?"

The young man looked up at her, squinting in the sun.

"Yes," he said.

"How much does it cost?" she asked.

"A long letter is 200 francs. A short letter is 100 francs."

She felt the corner of her scarf where she had tied up her coins. The bus home would cost 150 francs.

"A short letter," she said.

"Ok," he said. "Please sit."

He gave her the old wooden stool and sat on one of the steps of the post office. He got out his small box of pens and paper.

"Do you have an envelope and stamps?" he asked.

"No," she said.

"Where is the letter going?"

"France."

"A stamp is 75 francs. An envelope is 25 francs."

She thought and then said, "How much for a very short letter?"

"Still 100 francs."

She decided that she would walk home.

"Ok," she said.

"Do you have the address?"

She took a folded letter from her bra and gave it to the young man.

The young man took the folded letter and felt its dampness. It had a return address. He hesitated, but since the envelope was open, he took the letter out and glanced through it. It was from a man, the woman's fiancé, in Montpellier. It said that the fiancé had met another woman who was smart and who understood him. The other woman could speak French and read and write and had a car. The letter said that the woman in Mali was simple and traditional and uneducated. It said the fiancé needed someone more intelligent and who knew the world.

The young man looked at the woman. She was young, her hair was covered with a scarf, but he could see the neat ends of her braids slipping out. Her skin was smooth, glistening with sweat. She sat erect, motionless. Her face was still.

He wondered who had read the letter to her. He wondered if the reader had read exactly what the letter said.

"Ok," he said, taking out a sheet of paper, "what should the letter say?"

IN THE PARK

I love walking in the park with my daughter and grandkids. They are growing so fast. Sometimes I think I wouldn't recognize them the next time I see them.

We just walk around and chat. The kids play. We sit and watch the grandchildren play.

It can be quite noisy at times. Kids running around. A lot of confusion.

My daughter is talking with me.

"What a beautiful day," she says.

"Beautiful," I say. "So glad to be here."

"Do you want ta giber nash tadoon?' she asks.

"Sorry?"

"Do you thunk gibberkt ash doon?"

"Excuse me?"

"Want dis ard ta doon?"

"Maybe. Let me think…"

She looks confused. I am too, a bit.

I saw a woman at the park. She looked like the girl I had a crush on in high school. I can see her so vividly. The way she made me feel. I can visualize her but I can't quite remember her name. I think it starts with S or R. Sarah maybe.

Something like that. Or maybe Randy. Sarah Bernhardt? Hah, no that was a French actress.

anyway…

Someone asks me a question. No, is just talking excitedly. It is my granddaughter. The older one. The wild one. Her name is Suzie. Or Suzanne. She is talking about her friends, who I don't know, I think.

When we leave the park, my daughter goes in the wrong direction. But I go with them. Don't want to seem like a know-it-all.

It was Rachel. Her name was Rachel. The one in high school. She had long brown hair.

I love walking in the park with my daughter and her kids. They are growing so fast, I think I might not recognize them the next time I see them. I hope I can remember their names.

WHEN HER CAT SEES SNOW, OR, THERE IS A LOT OF PAPERWORK TO KILL YOURSELF

She has lung cancer. It is terminal. It is being treated. She is existing, barely. She has no children. She has a sister who is already dead. Her parents are dead, of course. Most of her friends are dead. The close ones anyway. She lives and works in Kuwait. She misses Ottawa.

She has a cat named Fred. It is a girl cat. Fixed. She wants to die.

Her, not the cat. On her terms. Maybe Fred too. Fred can be hard to fathom.

She has one wish to fulfill.

She is trying to get authorization for assisted suicide. Canada does this. They think that there are too many drawbacks to regular suicide. But regular suicide is an option. Regular suicide is a close second.

Who needs help to end their own life?

Somehow, there is a lot of paperwork to kill yourself. It should be simpler. They say authorization is beneficial for the disposition of assets. Whose assets? What assets? Anyway, she doesn't want to break the law by dying. That would be criminal. Rather die a criminal than live dead.

She thinks, who cares?

Fred.

In a very special way. But Fred is cool. Fred is Zen. Fred has no attachments. Fred is detached.

But Fred has never seen snow. Fred should get a chance to see snow. In Ottawa, Fred can see snow.

In Ottawa, Fred can also assist at the suicide.

NIGHT DRIVE

I got up early to go into town. Okandja was where I got supplies and picked up mail, and saw a buddy who was a volunteer there. Have a few beers. It was about an hour's drive through the rainforest on winding gravel roads. I did the trip every couple of weeks. I usually timed it with one of the biweekly flights from Libreville.

The trip was the same as usual. There were a few small villages with a couple of roadside stands—palm wine, game meat, manioc, bananas. The pickup cut out at kilometer 32 in a small dip in the road as it always did. I don't know why, but there was something going on at that spot.

When I got to town, kids came running up to the truck to tell me that Robbie was at the hospital. I stopped and asked them if he was okay and they said they thought so. I asked if it was malaria. They said they thought so. But he's okay? They thought so. I decided to do a couple of errands before stopping by the hospital.

I picked up my mail. Mainly some aerograms from my mom filled to the rim with her teacher's handwriting. At the end of the aerogram, she would always sign "Love, Ma. PS Your father says hi." I bought a case of sardines, batteries, kerosene, macaroni. I bought some illegal shotgun shells for Lucien. I got some perfume for Juliette.

When I got to the concrete block hospital, Robbie was sitting on a bed in a large room that had maybe 10 beds in it. I think there was one other patient. I sat across from Robbie on another bed. He seemed ok, but very subdued. I asked him how he was doing. He said okay. I asked whether it was malaria. He said maybe. While we were talking, the director of the school where Robbie taught came in. I knew him a bit. He was extremely agitated for some reason.

He said, "I'm glad you're here. You need to get Robbie to Libreville right now. Today's flight."

I said, "Okay. Okay. But Robbie seems to be doing okay. We don't have tickets for the flight and it leaves in 45 minutes."

The director said, "I don't care. Go to Robbie's house and get some clothes and get him on the plane. He has to leave today. He is not staying here. He can't stay here."

The director was determined and was not going to take "no" for an answer. I drove over to Robbie's house to get some clothes for him. His house was nice, but a cut-and-paste model teacher's house in a cleared area with a couple of other teacher houses. It was unlocked and I went in; it was like it always was, messy but welcoming. I went into the bedroom to look for clothes. There was a paper on the bed. It read: "Dear Mom and Pa, Dear Sis, I am really sorry, very sorry, but I just can't do it. I just can't go on another day..." My face got hot, the world stopped spinning, and everything froze. Everything froze. Everything was blurry. I put the note in my pocket. I found a bag and stuffed some clothes in it and went back to the hospital.

I picked up Robbie—I just grabbed him and said, "Come on, we're going." I drove like hell to the tiny airport—one small concrete building next to a gravel runway. The plane had already taxied down to the end of the runway and turned around, getting ready for take-off. It seemed to me that driving out onto the runway was the only choice I had, so I did. My truck and the plane face-to-face on the runway. I slowly drove down to the plane. When I was about 50 meters away, I got out and walked the rest of the way. One of the French pilots opened a cockpit window when I was close and asked what was going on. I said that I had a young American Peace Corps volunteer who had tried to kill himself and I needed to get him to Libreville. Luckily, the wife of one of the pilots worked at the Peace Corps. That eased the way. After some back and forth, they said they would take us.

I walked back to the truck, drove back to the "terminal" and parked the truck. Robbie and I walked out to the plane and boarded. We had two seats right behind the cockpit; crew seats, I think. We took off. As Robbie was sitting there, the pilot made some silent gestures trying to figure out how Robbie had tried to kill himself. Hanging? No. Slit wrist? No. I asked the pilot if he could call ahead and inform the Peace Corps and have someone pick us up at the airport in Libreville.

Two things I pieced together later. Robbie had tried to overdose on some medicines from the Peace Corps medical kit, and apparently, he had been shouting during the night about killing himself. Students and teachers had overheard and that's why the director was so agitated. Not for Robbie, but that he didn't want something bad to happen at his school.

Things finally slowed down on the plane. Robbie looked okay—just very subdued. At the time, I didn't know if he was coming or going. I didn't know really what to say. I just said, "Are you okay?" every once in a while. And he would say, "yeah." That was about it. I thought you don't say, "What a beautiful day," to someone who has just tried to kill themselves, and you don't say, "Life is fucked up either." So we just sat there mostly.

We got to Libreville and I thanked the pilots. We waited for the Peace Corps to show up. They never did. I got Robbie in a taxi and took him straight to the Peace Corps doctor's clinic. The doctor was a middle-aged Gabonese man, trained in the U.S., with perfect English. I explained to him what I knew and he asked Robbie a couple of questions and took him into a consulting room.

I took the taxi to the Peace Corps office. There I walked past everyone and went directly to the director's office.

He looked up from his desk and before I could say anything, he said, "Oh, so you're the one who's sick."

I said, "You got the message that a volunteer was in trouble and you didn't send anyone to the airport to pick them up?"

I took the suicide note from my pocket and, waving it, I said, "One of your volunteers has just tried to kill himself."

He took the note from me. I will always regret that I didn't keep the note. I wanted to give it back to Robbie.

The director immediately became more concerned about the situation. There was a lot of back and forth. And a long phone call was made to the doctor. The office was suddenly filled with energy. It appeared that Robbie was stable. He might have had his stomach pumped in Okandja. I never knew.

They decided that Robbie needed to be put on suicide watch, someone should be with him at all times, someone he knew and trusted. They thought I was the most appropriate person because I knew him best. I tried to argue that I had no training in this and didn't know what to do. They said, "All you have to do is be there and make sure he doesn't harm himself." As if that was easy. They insisted.

For several nights, I slept in the same room with Robbie. He took the bed and I took the floor. I don't think we slept much. Every so often, one of us would say, "Are you okay?" We talked about some other incidental stuff, day-to-day stuff, but avoided the big stuff.

Since I was in Libreville, the Peace Corps nurse thought it would be a good idea if I caught up with my vaccinations and shots. I went back to the doctor's office. They gave me a gamma globulin shot, which in those days was a 5 cc shot in the upper thigh. They did it one cc at a time with 5 m intervals between each push so that the vaccine could be absorbed by the thigh muscle. All the consultation rooms were occupied, so they had me sit in a large room, a nursery, where there were six cribs. I sat there, jeans around my ankles, no underwear, and a syringe in my thigh, watched by six Gabonese babies who were standing up in their cribs staring at me.

I met with the Peace Corps director.

"I suppose you want per diem," he said.

I said, "It's not a question of whether I want per diem but whether I deserve it."

I never got per diem.

After a few days, when Robbie was in the clear and arrangements were made for him to be repatriated, I also tried to return to my community. I said goodbye to Robbie. We stood outside the Peace Corps office in the sun, my ride waiting.

"Take care of yourself."

"Yeah, I will. You too."

"It'll work out. Things get better."

"Yeah, I know."

"There are a lot of things out there that are worth experiencing."

"Yeah."

"People care about you."

"Yeah."

"A lot to live for."

"Yeah, like not having to put up with your fucking snoring. Jesus."

"Fuck you. You think I enjoyed that?"

"And you smell like shit."

"Fuck off."

We shook hands.

The Peace Corps bought me a ticket, but the flights were full. I got a friend to take me to the airport anyway. The woman at the counter kept telling me to wait, that the flight was full. I never got a boarding pass. Finally, I just took my chance and walked by everyone out onto the tarmac. I walked up to the plane and there was a stewardess checking boarding passes at the foot of the steps. I smiled and just walked by. As I got to the top of the stairs, I realized that I might be in a bit of trouble if there were, in fact, no seats free. Luckily, there was one and I took it.

The plane made a stop in Lastoursville where I had some friends. They met the plane and I was scared to get off because they might not let me get back on without a boarding pass. From the top of the stairs, I chatted with Sam and Bill.

"We heard that Robbie tried to kill himself."

"Yeah."

"How did he do it?"

"Overdose."

"With what?"

"Not sure. Something from the medical kit."

"He's okay?"

"Yeah."

"Being sent home?"

"Yeah."

"Want a beer?"

"No, I'm good."

"Ok, see ya."

"Ok. Later."

It was late afternoon when I got to Okandja. The truck was there. The sardines, tomato paste, macaroni—everything was still in the bed of the truck.

The sun set and it was dark and cool on the drive home. No lights and no electricity for miles. I drove slowly with the windows down. Floating along the winding pitch black road, I felt I was in an eternal river, a black river with the stars above. My mind left my body and I floated above the truck. Below, two beams of light were searching for a way in the immense darkness.

THE TRUNK

The dusty road was the same: same turns, same dips, same washboard, same times. There were the same villages, same markets—maybe larger now. It was the same, only more. More of the same.

In Farabana, there were new houses, but the same style, same sizes. Just more. The roadside vendors were selling the same things, same small piles of tomatoes, the local eggplants, the same bowls of millet, the same soumbala, the same, and the same.

He recognized Amadou's house. It was the same. They sat outside under a straw hangar to escape the heat. Low stools and the same string chairs. The inevitable group of kids, different, but the same.

Proudly, Amadou and his brother brought the trunk he'd left there out from the bedroom and placed it, like a casket at a viewing, in the center of the group under the hangar. Both he and Amadou had long since lost the keys to the padlock. They called a metal worker from the market to come and saw it off. This took some time.

They sat around anxiously as he eventually opened it.

The contents were as follows:

Books: There were 22.

Fiction: Cry the Beloved Country—Paton; Cannery Row—Steinbeck; Things Fall Apart—Achebe; The Fountainhead—Rand; Leaves of Grass—Whitman; Heart of Darkness—Conrad; The Fire Next Time—Baldwin; The Wretched of the Earth—Fanon; On the Road—Kerouac; Pedagogy of the Oppressed—Freire; Bound to Violence—Ouologuem; A Bend in the River—Naipaul; Zen and the Art of Motorcycle Maintenance—Pirsig; Trout Fishing in America—Brautigan; Omoo—Melville.

Non-fiction: Handbook of Tropical Diseases; The Mammals of Africa, The Birds of Africa, Tropical Crops—Monocotyledons; Reforestation in Arid Lands; Small Scale Poultry Keeping; Raising Turkeys for Fun and Profit.

Cassettes: There were 15. These included Hendrix, Joplin, The Doors, The Stones, The Who, The Temptations, The Supremes, Sam and Dave, Richard Pryor, James Taylor, John Mayall, Stevie Winwood, Howlin' Wolf, Muddy Waters, and Cream.

Stationery and written material: There were five notebooks (one empty, one full and three half-filled in with notes), blue folding prepaid airmail envelopes, a bundle of letters (most appeared to be from his mother, a couple from his sister, a couple from high school friends, one or two from his father, and the Dear John letter from Sarah).

There were no pens. He must have given them away.

Clothes: There were four t-shirts, worn, two black, one white, one yellow; two jeans, worn; four boxers, worn; black

Converse high tops—worn out; blue flip flops; three pairs white gym socks.

Sundry: A needle for a basketball pump; a long knife (he immediately gave this to Amadou, explaining that he would have no use for it in the States); an axe (ditto); a key chain; an inner tube repair kit; a first aid kit—mostly emptied out with some bandages left; a flashlight (he must have given his storm lamp away); two can openers; some assorted silverware; three ceramic covered metal bowls; three ceramic covered metal coffee cups.

He looked down at the trunk and its contents, trying to recreate the person who owned it. A young, idealistic person had owned these things. A person who did not care too much for appearances. A person who wanted to do good in the world. But he was not sure how he knew this. It was him, but a different him from long ago. He was neither ashamed nor proud of what this was. His history, a small, insignificant history.

He wanted to tell Amadou to just keep the trunk, but he realized Amadou might be hurt after all the effort he made to preserve it.

He hugged Amadou and thanked him for keeping the trunk.

On the way back to Lomé, he stopped next to the Okomo River, added some stones to the trunk, and threw it off the Mayumba Bridge.

STELLA

They lifted their glasses.

"To Stella, wishing she were here."

"If she was here, she would chew us out. Royally."

"Yeah. She would say, 'don't waste everyone's time, go out and do something useful.'"

For the past 8 years, Frank and Mike had met, or tried to meet, as close to March 19th as they could. Sometimes it was in the Boston area, sometimes in DC. Once in New York. This time, they were in Washington. Mike was down for a conference. They met at Lucky's on 14th street. They sat in a dark booth at the back of the bar and got a pitcher of *Modelo*.

Mike was a well-traveled PhD student originally from the Democratic Republic of the Congo. He had known Stella for many years before they had met Frank. They caught up a bit. But the talk of Stella could not be contained. March 19th was the anniversary of the day she died.

Frank worked for a development consulting company in Washington. When Frank had first met Stella, she had come down from Boston to work on the analysis of the field survey data that Frank's project had collected. She barely gave him the time of day. He said to himself, "This person is a very good judge of character."

Six months later, he went to Boston to teach at her university for a semester. They shared an office in an old, run-down building. Slowly, they became friends. But he thought, "This person has lowered their standards a lot."

Frank and Stella would talk about development and Development. Frank had just been introduced to the work of Foucault and she would sympathize with his bewilderment. They became gym buddies. Every Thursday, they would go to Ace Liquors and get a bottle of wine and then go to the sushi place and sit and talk and eat.

That was when he also became friends with Mike. Mike was also at the university, working on his PhD. They were all passionate about development and Africa. They co-led a course lab.

Toward the end of the semester, she had decided to go back to Kenya. Her mom wasn't well and was getting older.

Stella had just gotten back from field interviews outside of Nairobi. He had gotten messages from her saying that she was not feeling well, could not climb the stairs in her mom's house. He felt that she might need money, and sent some by Western Union. He pleaded with her to go and see a doctor.

Eight years later he still had the messages on his phone. As part of the yearly ritual, he showed them to Mike.

> Frank: ok just let me know how you are doing that's all

> Stella: Ok I will. I'll go to the doctor first thing. I'll try not to die tonight. Lol. Terrible joke.

And she had died that night.

Frank got the call from Mike early the next day. Frank couldn't concentrate. They cried over the phone. Frank was in Dakar. Like a movie cliché, he took a long walk on the beach. He did not know what else to do.

He could not go to the funeral outside of Nairobi, but Mike did. Mike sent back pictures. The funeral involved dancing. Of all the things of Stella's that her mom could have carried while dancing; the jewelry, the books, the pictures; she carried Stella's PhD diploma.

Later, at the ceremony at the university, they sat in a conference room in the old rundown building. People spoke. The question was freqently, "why?" Her death had to mean something. It could not be the result of a senseless and indifferent universe. Why her? Why now?

After sipping his beer, Mike said, "After these years, I still am bothered by how senseless it seems. In my head, I just hear why? Why? Why?"

"Yeah, it seems so unjust. So unfair. Or so arbitrary."

"Such a meaningless thing should not have happened to one so bright and full of life."

"Certainly, from the bigger picture—from the infinite space of the universe or the endlessness of eternity, it doesn't seem to matter. Just a butterfly flapping its wings."

"Yes, but you know the butterfly effect. A butterfly flaps its wings in Patagonia and it influences a cyclone in Madagascar."

"Yeah, but does it? I mean, time and space don't seem to have changed at all."

"But hard for us to know."

"But maybe meaning depends on scale. That it doesn't seem to matter to the universe, still pretty important for the butterfly…"

"And her friends."

"And her friends. You know. Clearly meaningless or clearly so infinitesimal as to be meaningless at the scale of the universe, but at our scale, here on earth, in this bar, for you and me, maybe it has meaning."

"Cheers. I'll drink to that."

"No, I mean it. Maybe at large-scale meaning disappears. Or maybe within a meaningless universe, the fact that meaning can exist on a human scale is not a contradiction. Like quantum physics and normal physics existing together, although they seem like a contradiction. Depends on scale. The dominant forces at the universal level are not the dominant forces at the human level."

"Ok, so how about this one: Is meaning a feeling or a fact? Is it subjective or objective?"

"Is both an option?"

"No."

"Is neither an option?"

"No."

"Is that really a fair question?"

"I don't know, but answer it anyway."

"So a fact is something that is objectively verifiable, and a feeling is subjective?"

"More or less."

"Do you need society's concurrence to find meaning? I don't think so. You can find it on your own. You don't need validation."

"But do you find it or do you create it?"

"It certainly feels like you should find it."

"But do you really?"

"Ok, suppose you create it. Why does that feel cheap and superficial and arbitrary almost?"

"Because you are always looking for validation outside of yourself. We're programmed like that."

"Okay, so how about this one—can meaning be temporary or must it be permanent?"

"Again, is both an option?"

"No. And neither is neither. You have to choose."

"If it was permanent, it would really clutter up the universe. All these meanings never changing. Growth depends on death. Gotta go with temporary."

"Yeah. Temporary. Scale-dependent. Subjective."

They ordered another pitcher and a plate of wings. The place was emptying out. The happy hour crowd was leaving.

Frank said, "So if it's true that meaning can exist in a meaningless world, and that it can be subjective and temporary, what is the meaning of Stella's death? Aren't we better off struggling with the fact that it might be meaningless instead of trying to assign some faulty meaning to it?"

"It's not faulty if it makes a difference."

"That meaning is created, it's not discovered."

"And that's our job."

"Okay. Let's do our job. What is the meaning of Stella's death for you?"

"We need more drinks."

"Maybe meaning depends on how much you've had to drink."

"Cheers!"

They ordered another round and waited for it to come. Lucky's was dark and growing quiet. The floor was varnished with a thousand spilt beers.

Frank said, "Okay. I'll go first. Stella was a wonderful, bright, beautiful butterfly. Hard to catch butterflies by chasing them. You got to tend your own garden for them to come. So part of the meaning of her death is that we need to do the best we can at what we are best at, and let the universe shake it out. That the universe might not care is not our problem. Doing what we can to make this specific place, this time, the best it can be."

"I can buy that."

"You got your own meaning? You can't steal mine."

Mike took a long drink of beer.

"Ok. For me, the message is that every day is a gift—don't squander it. Don't waste your time on trivial shit," Mike said.

"Like what?"

"Like regrets. Like jealousy. Like gossip. Like small thoughts. Like fear."

"Like your phone."

"Like your phone."

"Go big, like she did."

They talked more. Mike described the conference he was attending.

"I gotta go. I got a presentation tomorrow," he said.

They came out of the bar to the cool of the night.

"Next year."

"Next year, if not before."

They hugged and Mike went off toward his hotel and Frank went the other direction to the metro station.

Frank came up out of the subway at DuPont and walked through the circle. It was dark and the circle was almost empty. A couple walking. A homeless man sleeping. The stars were bright above. The wind picked up just slightly.

"Jesus," he thought, "That damn butterfly is still disturbing the universe."

THE MUD HOUSE

He rented a mud house in the community. Other people would say he rented a mud hut in the village. But these terms are packed with pejoration and condescension. Like many communities in the world, there was no electricity and no running water. The house was owned by Oberabélé. She had a series of 5 houses in a gentle arc on a bare piece of ground between the road and the forest. She and her kids and sisters lived in the other 4 houses. His rent was $9 a month. Flashlights and a kerosene storm lamp were the only source of light in the house. He kept a bottle of water near his bed. Like everyone else, he went into the forest to take care of his needs. He washed from a bucket behind the house.

Oberabélé was an immaculate dresser. Every time she went out, she was washed and her clothes were clean and ironed. Beads of sweat were adornments and not exceptions. Even in the heat, she kept her balance. She was his "landlady" and advisor. Oberabélé did not seem to have a husband, at least one that was in the community. She seemed to have several young children, but it was hard to tell which ones were hers, which ones she had responsibility for, and which ones just hung out in the compound.

The house had two small rooms with a thatched roof. The back room was the bedroom. The front room had two low chairs, a low table, and a trunk. The house had a roughhewn wooden door and two small wooden windows. It was made without power tools, levels, or T-squares, like an outgrowth of the earth. No screens and no glass. The floor and yard were packed dirt, frequently swept.

He had built a bed frame that was higher off the ground than most beds. He had a slight fear of snakes and ants. A foam mattress sat on top of the frame. A small bed table held the flashlight, storm lamp, bottle of water, and books.

He spent endless nights in the hut surrounded by darkness and heat.

The house was alive. At first, this bothered him and kept him up. Many nights, he lay awake listening to the hunts and the courtships in the thatch above. He was just another part of the ecosystem.

Frequently, in the dead dark of night, something small, in the grips of death or love, would drop, in agony or ecstasy, from the thatch onto the bed. Many times it would freeze for a second while he wondered whether it was a snake with a mouse, or two giant millipedes coupled. Or maybe it was just a gecko that lost its footing. Whatever it was, it was always gone before the beam of his flashlight made it in their direction. The house had all this. And he came to accept it.

Once he awoke in the middle of the night. He heard some low talking outside but this was usual. He decided that he might as well get up and pee. He swung his feet off of the bed and as soon as his feet touched the ground, he felt something pinch; once, twice, several times. He turned on the flashlight and saw thousands of ants on the dirt floor. They were everywhere. He quickly exited the house and, in the moonlight, saw other people in their yards. In fact, most of the people in his neighborhood seemed to be out. A huge column of army ants was going through this part of town. Luckily, his house was on the edge of the column and not where the ants were the densest. He was confused and asked Oberabélé what he should do. She said there is nothing to do. Just get out of the way, be patient and wait. They are not interested in you.

In a few hours, they were gone.

-o-o-o-o-o-

Sometimes he thought of the house as a telephone booth. You went in and you got the message and once you got the message, you left.

Sometimes it was like a spaceship to Mars. You went in and you went to sleep and after several months, you woke up on a different planet.

Sometimes it was a trap, a snare. You got caught and couldn't escape.

Sometimes it was like a classroom. You went in and sat down, and learned if you were able to pay attention.

Sometimes it was like a prison. You just waited for your time to be done and to get out.

Sometimes he felt it was like a computer program. Garbage in, garbage out.

Sometimes the house was a coffin. You died there and stayed an eternity.

Sometimes it was like an airplane black box. It recorded the last events before the fatal crash.

Sometimes he thought of the house as like an incubator. You went in as something and you came out as something else.

Sometimes it seemed like a cocoon. You crawled in as a caterpillar and you emerged as a dusty moth. Or a cockroach.

And maybe it was like a mud oven.

"It sometimes feels as though I've been baked, transformed, mutated. Like the hut was an oven," he said.

"Half-baked," his friend said.

"No, I've been in there a long time. I've come out a different person from when I went in."

"Temp and duration matter," said his friend. "But you still need the right flour and yeast to make a good loaf."

"Yeah, but at this point, flour and yeast are a given. The only things you can play with are temperature and time."

And other things that did not enter his consciousness at that time. It was just home.

OBERABÉLÉ

They were talking about their village landladies. He mentioned that his was named "Oberabélé."

"Interesting name," the other said. "What's it mean?"

"I don't know. It's just a name, I guess."

"Just a name?" the other said. "There isn't just 'just a name' here. It's not like John or Paul. Every name has a meaning."

He had rented a hut from her for 18 months. Back in the village, at night, squatting around the cooking fire, he asked her what Oberabélé meant. The night was clear and warm. She wore a t-shirt and a *pagne*.

She said, "The one who brought me here is gone."

ACKNOWLEDGEMENTS

Steve Altman

The Bear Mountain Writers

Asif Shaikh

Lisa Anderson

Howard Anderson

Deb Kreutzer

Sally Anderson

MG

Zach Davis

Oberabélé

The Inner Loop

Fellow passengers and travelers through life in Gabon, Mali, Senegal, Ghana, Tanzania, Kenya, Madagascar, Namibia, Botswana, USA, and points beyond.

BIOGRAPHY

Jon Anderson is committed to helping the voiceless find expression, and promoting under-represented views, including through writing. One of his favorite biological processes is fermentation. He lives in Washington, DC.

"All This," "Nafissa," "Almost Perfect", and "They Think" appeared as Mali Quartet in Fluent Winter 2016 Volume 4 No 3

"The Letter Writer" appeared in Quail Bell on December 29, 2016

"The Green Shoes" appeared in Quail Bell on January 4, 2017

"A Servant of Peace" and "Notes from the Cat Sitter" first appeared in Unhinged Magazine

"Five Birds" appeared in Flash Fiction Magazine on July 4, 2017

"Mushroom Risotto" appeared in Fluent Spring 2017 Volume 5 No2

"The Woman and the Writer" appeared in District Lit

9 7 9 8 9 9 9 3 6 4 6 1 0 7